CHANCE

Sara McAulay

CHANCE

Alfred A. Knopf   New York   1982

THIS IS A BORZOI BOOK
PUBLISHED BY ALFRED A. KNOPF, INC.

Library of Congress Cataloging in Publication Data
McAulay, Sara.
Chance.   I. Title.
PS3563.C33C47   1982   813'.54   81-15664
ISBN 0-394-51869-1   AACR2

Manufactured in the United States of America
First Edition

To the memory of my mother

CHANCE

1

THE ROAD snakes uphill, mostly clear of snow but wet, with icy patches glittering in the headlights' beam. Yellow reflectors wink on the metal stakes along the shoulder; guardrail just a thin wire ribbon between the pink Mustang and a long ways down. The girl doesn't care. She keeps her foot on the gas and cranks the wheel, sliding the car through the turns like Bobby Allison at Daytona, or A. J. Foyt. Chance would be proud of her. If she breathes carefully—little shallow panting breaths that whistle past her teeth—the burning in her lungs is not too bad. The secret is not to cough.

Up ahead are the turnout and the parking lot, and the fire trail that hasn't been used in years. Rutted, gullied, barely wider than the car, it's studded with rocks, laced with exposed roots half hidden under the snow. Branches slap at the windshield and scrape along the doors, digging up paint. The Mustang bucks and wallows. Its springs creak. Every so often the bellypan slams down—*thunk!*—on a boulder or a sawed-off stump. The girl pays no attention. She breathes carefully through her teeth. Shoving the lever into low, she drives on down through the switchbacks to the canyon floor at the foot of the ridge and then up out of the canyon on the other side.

It doesn't occur to her that she might get stuck; it doesn't cross her mind that she might not be able to get where she wants to go. Her lungs burn, but it is not too bad and she keeps her foot on the gas and twirls the power steering this way and that while the engine roars and the tires howl as they spin. Rocks and mud and snow splat against the car's steel belly as the headlights poke crazily into dark spaces between trees. Once, a pair of brilliant green eyes glow out at her from somewhere deep in the pines.

From the top of that ridge the trail winds down and then up again, rougher and fainter and harder to follow, until it finally ends on a barren rocky bluff. Shivering, the girl zips her jacket higher under her chin and steps out of the car. The wind is fiercely cold and has swept the bluff almost clean of snow. The Mustang's headlights fan out into the darkness, showing her nothing. She has no way of telling whether she has arrived at the Copper Creek canyon or the edge of the world. But then the clouds break apart, spilling moonlight into the canyon below. Water shines darkly, a long curving band of it like tarnished metal, and the snowy meadow on its far side glows for a moment, an eerie, icy blue. The girl can't see the cabin but she knows exactly where it is, back in the trees against the canyon's western wall.

Chance? she says, and cocks her head to listen. Wind in the trees, the rasping of her breath. And then his voice: Didn't I tell you? Sugar, didn't I tell you it was fine?

I knew you'd be here, she says, I knew I'd find you, I just wasn't looking in the right place, before.

And it's true; he is here. He is all around, in the hazy moonlight filtering through the trees and in the skeletal black branches and the frozen brittle weeds and muddy stones. The girl breathes carefully, shallow little breaths that dry her teeth and tongue. I'm going to take care of it, she says, and shows him the gun.

He laughs. Sugar, you got to be kidding.

I'm not kidding, she tells him. I'm going to take care of it, that's all.

She stands there for fifteen minutes or so, turning the gun in her hand and staring down at the trees that hide the cabin. Then the clouds come together again, pinching off the shafts of moonlight one by one, leaving the canyon in darkness broken only by the faint wink and flicker of the creek. Chance? she says. No answer; the moonlight has taken him. But he will be back.

She settles down to wait out the night in the Mustang, wrapped in an old ripped beach towel she finds in the trunk under the spare. Her head pounds and her throat has swollen almost closed, but the burning in her lungs is not too bad. She clenches her teeth and her breath whistles through them, louder than the wind whistles through the branches of the pines behind the car. Every so often a fit of shivering takes her, jerks her up straight and wide-eyed for a moment and then turns her loose again. But the secret is not to cough. As long as she doesn't cough she'll be okay.

Off and on during the night she sleeps, and she fiddles with the radio. Station from Salt Lake: the Mormon Tabernacle Choir. Disco from Vegas, blues from somewhere, some kind of symphony. Way down at the bottom of the dial she finds some country but the reception is poor: Waylon Jennings fading in and out, his voice full of crackles and whistles and the slopover from some other station's news. The girl doesn't care. She isn't really listening anyway. She clutches the gun. The clouds have rolled back, the moonlight pours down. He tells her, Sugar, you got to be kidding. You can't do the job with just that little toy.

She throws open the car door: *Chance?* But the wind burns her eyes and the clouds gather again and he is gone. "I'm going to do it," she says aloud. "One way or another, I'll get it done."

2

IT WAS 2 A.M. when the bus rolled into Cresta. The girl had been dozing for an hour or more; now she sat up straight and rubbed a clear patch on the steamy window. Wet shining street, nearly empty, cafes and bars on either side. Dew Drop Inn, Pair-O-Dice Alley, The Lace Garter. Neon signs fuzzy in the rain. She could make out the shapes of slot machines behind the smeared glass of the depot door, and the sign above the door that said, in scabby gold, CRESTA, NEV. POP 3200, ELEV 4896. A jeep and two crew-cab pickups stood at the curb in front of The Lace Garter, their rear windows barred with racked guns. Best hunting in the world, he used to tell her. Everything from jackrabbits to six-point bucks, just name your game. She closed her eyes, pretending for a moment that she wasn't getting off.

The driver said, "Well, miss, this is it."

"Guess so." She stood up—a big girl, squarely built and maybe twenty years old, with a broad-jawed face heavily and inexpertly made up, and a frizz of yellow hair. "Yeah, this looks like my stop, all right." From the south somewhere. A country girl. She zipped her white vinyl jacket and slung a black patent purse over her shoulder. "Thanks," she said.

Then, dragging her suitcase, she stepped off the bus into the slanting rain.

The depot was almost deserted—nobody home but the dispatcher and a colored guy asleep on a bench with a newspaper over his face. The girl set her suitcase down beside one of the slot machines and approached the desk, where the dispatcher was eating a banana. His hair was gray, his eyes light-colored, tired, with pouchy lashless lids. He glanced at the girl. "Cold enough for you?"

"Pretty near." At one of the stops she'd heard a trucker say there was snow on Thomson Pass, wherever that was, and she could well believe it. She looked around, studying the place, studying the two men out of the corner of her eye, already beginning to sweat.

The dispatcher finished his banana and folded the skin into a neat little package. They were overdue for some weather, he remarked. "This little storm ain't much, for the middle of November. Gets colder'n sin around here sometimes, specially up in the high country." He paused, regarding her with his light-colored eyes that were neither blue nor gray nor tan, poking his back teeth with the tip of his tongue. The girl waited, saying nothing, sweat itching between her shoulder blades. "Backpackers freeze to death up there sometimes," the dispatcher said. "It can happen, even in September, and that's God's own truth. But I don't guess you're here to go backpacking."

The girl looked down at her flimsy needle-heeled boots and shook her head. "I guess not."

"I guess not," he said, and picked up a dog-eared *Field & Stream*.

The girl rummaged in her purse, came up with a dime and thumbed it into the nearest slot machine. She didn't pull the handle right away. Go on, sugar, close your eyes; hold your nose and jump, he'd say. But she knew better. Some things it didn't pay to hurry.

She glanced sidelong at the two men again. Perhaps he had known them. Or they had known him. Known of him: *Chance Griffin? Ain't he the one who left here and went on to be a famous jockey? Didn't he use to ride for Mr. French?* Famous jockey. That's how they'd still think of him in Cresta. It was possible. Anything was possible, now that she was here. It was even possible that he had stood right where she was standing now, his hand on the lever of this very machine.

The back of her neck prickled. She listened to the black man's gentle snores, heard the rustle of the dispatcher's magazine as he turned a page; she took a breath, held it and slammed the handle down. Cherries, lemon, plum. Three dimes rattled into the cup. She played them back the way he would have done, and when they were gone she swallowed and wiped her hands on the seat of her orange jeans. It wasn't Chance she should be thinking about now. "Maybe you could help me," she said to the dispatcher. "I'm looking for a guy."

"Yeah?" The dispatcher lowered his magazine and raised a sparse gray eyebrow. "Who?"

The girl played another dime. Her mouth had gone dry; her upper lip clung to her teeth. The man on the bench snored gently and steadily, one hand trailing on the cracked brown lino floor. And there were fans in the ceiling, she noted suddenly. Big brown three-bladed fans. Two of them. Not turning, of course, not in this weather. But she should have spotted them sooner.

She frowned, willing her lip down over her teeth. "Well, see, there's a problem. I had his name and phone number and all, everything wrote down in my little book. But looks like I lost it." She licked her teeth before she tried a smile. "Dumb, huh?"

Amazing, really—amazing and a little scary too—how easy

it was, how quickly it all came back. *Mama says please can we pay you next week?* while back at the house Mama's halfway packed already, stuff crammed in boxes, the old Hudson pulled up close to the kitchen door. *Next week for sure, Mr. Gomez. I promise!* The girl smiled again, more easily, and said to the dispatcher, "You ever hear of anything so dumb?"

The dispatcher shrugged and reopened his magazine.

"Story of my life," plaintively, feeding yet another dime into the machine. "All I know is this is the right town to get off at, and the guy's rich and he owns a big ranch near here somewhere." She pulled the lever: plum, plum, orange. "Snake eyes. Wouldn't you know. You got any idea who it could be?"

The black man sat up then, squinting and blinking and rubbing his eyes. His skin was dark but his hair was a rusty red. He reminded the girl of someone but she couldn't think who. She put a dollar on the desk and asked the dispatcher for change, watching as the other man deftly rolled a cigarette. She couldn't tell if he'd been listening or not.

"You got business with this guy?" The dispatcher winked at the redhead and both men grinned. The girl stared them down. Then she said, "I'm a waitress," and turned back to the machine. She glanced at the coins in her hand, selected one, discarded it, chose another and eased it into the slot. "Must be some trick to this." She shrugged. "Tell you the truth, though, I'm temporarily between jobs right now, and I heard there's this guy around here who's supposed to be throwing a big party pretty soon."

She waited, feeling their eyes on her, crawling over her like bugs. *Find out what they want.* Mama used to say that. *Find out what they want, and be it.* No way! She'd said waitress but they thought hooker; she could see it in their eyes as they checked out the Passion Plum nail polish, the Nile Temptress eye shadow, greeny-gold bracelets and rings picked special to go with the boots and the purse, the orange jeans and the white vinyl jacket with the curled stiff lapels. She'd gotten the idea from that undercover cop, the Master of Disguises, that she'd seen on Johnny Carson, and you had to admit it was slick. A new name, a whole new personality, the farthest from your own, that you could put on and take off like a coat. Only the suitcase was wrong—scuffed and peeling, held shut with twine. But it had been his.

She crossed her fingers. "Come on now," leaning into the handle. "Gimme a break." She had quit sweating. The machine whirred and then clanked to a stop. "Damn." She grinned ruefully, showing a lipstick-stained tooth. "Some days, seems like you can't come up no way but empty."

"Don't call 'em bandits for nothing," the dispatcher agreed, and the other man asked what kind of party.

"Real exclusive," the girl said, and shrugged again. "That's what I heard. Some real wealthy guy likes to throw parties at the end of deer season or something, and he might be hiring." She hesitated, jingling dimes in her palm. "Waitresses and bartenders and like that."

The two men traded looks and the girl frowned, jingling the coins. "Here I've come all the way up from Phoenix and can't even remember his name. What a dummy."

The red-haired man scratched his head, digging at his scalp with nails as yellow and thick as lemon rind. "Hey Jack," to the dispatcher. "You don't spose she's talking about Lou French."

The girl didn't move a muscle. She stared at the flyspecked vacation poster on the wall above the slot machine. Crown Pacific Cruises, it said; the white ship strung with colored lights, steaming out of Galveston. *My daddy is too the captain!* and then Chance's voice, faint but clear: "Sugar, how'd you like to go . . . ?" His smile's like a picket gate since the accident last fall but he doesn't care. Two races that afternoon, forty laps each around the muddy little oval, and he won them both, laying the bike over in the turns, scraping the track with a steel-soled boot. Both times Ellen had clambered over people's legs, saying "scuse me, scuse me," on her way down from the grandstand where he'd told her to sit so she could see, and both times she was too late to have her picture taken with him. But the second time he let her wheel the Suzuki back to the truck so that he could go off up the hill with Lou French, the two of them talking—or rather, Lou French talking and Chance nodding his head. And then Chance came back to the truck alone. "Sugar, how'd you like us to go down to Richmond and work for my buddy Lou?"

The girl stared at the poster until the blue-green waves and the blue-blue sky and the clean white ship with its crowd of suntanned people all blurred and ran together, and she didn't move and her expression didn't change. "More than likely it's Stan Jensen," the dispatcher was saying. "Old Stan, he likes the ladies. Hell, it could be anybody, any one of a dozen different guys." He laughed. "Don't I wish it was me!"

"Lou French," she said hesitantly. Her voice threatened to catch; a nerve jumped in her cheek. She closed her eyes for a moment, breathed in deeply and went on. "That could be him, I guess. Is he rich?"

The dispatcher laughed again. "You better believe! He's got a five-thousand-acre spread outside of town ten miles or so, and another big place back east. Owns racehorses and sailing yachts and a Lear jet."

"Dude's got ten fingers and a whole bakery full of pies," the black man said, and winked at her. "Ain't that so, Jack? I hear he give out Cadillacs on Halloween, for trick or treat. Girl, you better hope he's the one."

"Yeah, but waitresses?" The dispatcher folded his magazine, his face suddenly doubtful. You could tell that waitress wasn't what he meant. "Miss, if you'll pardon me saying it, I think you got the wrong guy."

"Can't be the wrong guy." She made her smile eager; her

eyes were wide and very bright beneath the heavy black lashes and the crescents of Nile Temptress. "It's him! Lou French, that's the name all right. I remember now."

The dispatcher said stubbornly, "It don't make sense."

"Why not?" asked the other man. "He's here now, ain't he? Him and about a dozen guests."

The dispatcher rolled his eyes and looked pained. "They're up to the lodge, Harry, you know they are. No place up there for girls like that!"

Harry pointed out that Lou French and his guests had to come down off the mountain sometime. And they always had a party when they did. Every year; it was a tradition. Everyone knew that. "Man, my brother tended bar for him last year, and he told me they had girls swinging from the rafters."

"I don't swing from rafters." She spoke softly, but they heard. "I'm a cocktail waitress, which for your information is a perfectly respectable job. And if there ain't anything like that available I'm moving on. But I'm not going nowhere till I know."

The two men looked at each other. The dispatcher pursed his lips as if he might whistle. The girl lifted her chin. "And if there ain't no job that Lou French guy can tell me so himself. I don't have to listen to hearsay."

"You want to talk to Mr. French, you're going to have to wait," the dispatcher told her. "Like I said, they're all up to the lodge, way up near the treeline. I speck they'll be there awhile, too."

The starch seemed to go out of her then. She steadied herself with one hand on the bandit's chrome flank and shook her head wearily. "Snake eyes again. I can't deal with this. I mean, eight hours on the damn bus and the guy ain't even *here?*" Her voice wavered. "What am I supposed to do now?"

There was a hotel just around the corner a couple blocks,

the dispatcher said. Not fancy, but the beds were clean. "You
got any money?"

"Some."

"Get some rest," he told her kindly. "Get a good night's
sleep and think it over when you get up. There's a bus going
south out of here at noon."

"Noon." She nodded slowly. "If I don't oversleep. But if I
do decide to stick around, I guess I won't have any trouble
finding Mr. French's place, will I?"

The dispatcher said no, the Double Deuce was a big ranch.
It was right there on Route 212, ten miles west of town. There
was a sign; she couldn't miss it blindfolded. She'd have to find
her own way out and back, though, he added. "This ain't
Reno, miss. We don't run local transit."

"Okay." She nodded soberly. "Well, thanks for your help."
As she bent to pick up her suitcase she saw a face mirrored
in the curved chrome of the slot machine's side. Cheap-looking
two-bottle blonde; clown suit and warpaint. Cocktail waitress,
hooker, find out what they want and be it. Oh Jesus God,
she thought. I'm nobody I'd even want to meet.

The Aberdeen Hotel wasn't fancy but it was cheap and the
desk clerk who took the girl's money didn't seem to find anything
unusual about her clothes or hair or the fact that it was after
three o'clock by that time, the bus long gone and the town
with its sidewalks rolled. All he asked was sixteen fifty, cash
in advance. She paid for three nights and, after a moment's
hesitation, signed the register in a round, schoolgirlish hand.
Helen Flynn, she wrote. It was, she realized later, a good deal
closer to the truth than was really smart.

Her room was on the third floor. Bed, straight chair, dresser.
Thin tweedy carpet worn bald near the door and in front of
the closet. Bathrooms down an ill-lit corridor. Just a room like

a lot of other rooms and better than some; it shouldn't have bothered her. But she was exhausted from five days on the road, from watching over her shoulder, from thinking three jumps ahead, or trying to: clothes from the Charles Town Salvation Army, hair job in the Greyhound restroom in Kansas City and no way of knowing if Lou French had changed his plans. Her head ached, her throat felt scratchy; a cold coming on? And for sure she could have done without the picture on the wall above the dresser.

Two cowboys. They were painted in electrified-looking colors that, she decided, would probably glow in the dark. One of the men lay in the yellow dust under an orange sky, green cactus and purple flat-topped hills in the distance, while the other one stood over him, smiling and blowing the smoke out of the barrel of his forty-five. A fancy brass plaque in the frame said, *Frontier Justice*.

The girl took the picture down and leaned it with its face against the wall, but she could still see it. Even when she closed her eyes the dead cowboy still sprawled there, thin-legged and awkward on the dry bare ground, his hat knocked off and a brilliant red stain spreading across his shirt. And the other one smiled grimly down and blew across the end of his gun barrel like he was playing a tune on a bottle.

She bought a Coke from the machine at the end of the hall, swallowed four aspirin and then, with her suitcase still unopened on the bed, stationed herself at the window, absently twisting the little wooden horse head on its chain around her neck while she stared out through the rain at the street below. A stray dog nosed among soggy cardboard cartons in front of a dark cafe. A real interesting sight, she told herself; stay awake, stay awake, you wouldn't want to miss it.

She should have given up. She was tired enough that she was seeing double; her teeth had suddenly begun to chatter, her head throbbed and the bed was clean, after all—or looked clean, which was pretty much the same thing as far as she was concerned. Even the chair would have been okay. You can sleep comfortably, peacefully, on a chair; she'd done it many a time, usually in somebody's kitchen with somebody's old hound at her feet, half-hearing and half-dreaming the soft slap of the cards on the table or the rattle of dice and the men's harsh laughter as the bottle went around. The chair would have been fine. But she stayed where she was, staring out the window at the rain, and then through the rain into clear warm sunshine, a summer afternoon somewhere sometime, she and Chance walking along the edge of a high steep cliff. It is no cliff that she knows, no place that she has ever been, yet it seems familiar, as if they have walked there together many times. Still, she doesn't know what lies at the bottom of the cliff. Water? Rocks? Whatever, it's a very long way down. And Chance walks between her and the edge. It is his way; good manners, he explains. He was brought up to treat the ladies right. So he walks between her and the edge of the cliff, sun on their shoulders and the grass thick and springy underfoot, and then without warning the cliff crumbles, the edge breaks away, and Chance pitches away from her, sideways and down.

Somehow she manages to grab one of his hands. A good grip; they clasp each other's wrists and she lies face down in the deep springy grass, free arm braced, legs wide, digging in with the toes of her shoes, her fingernails, her nose her chin her teeth while he swings, twisting and kicking like a rabbit in a snare, high above the sharp rocks, the cold ocean, the bottomless well.

And then she is falling too. Beginning to fall; inch by inch sliding toward the edge, bits of the edge crumbling and falling away. His weight pulls her. Slight as he is, she can't hold him, can't pull him to safety, is powerless to stop her own slide toward the edge. So she opens her hand. Lets go of his wrist. But he holds her with steel fingers and she continues to slide; the smell of damp earth and crushed grass, tiny blades straightening one by one just inches from her face. The edge crumbles, her free hand gropes at nothing; in terror she wrenches loose from his grasp. She shakes him off with a sudden violent jerk of her arm, as though he were a bug that had crawled onto her hand, and he falls and she is safe, lying face down in the soft bruised-smelling grass.

The dog was still there by the empty boxes. What was left of her Coke was still cold. She'd only slept for ten minutes or so, but ten minutes were more than enough. Five would do it. Three. She'd had that dream before, a dozen times at least; it left her helpless, angry and confused. She knew she couldn't have saved him, neither from falling nor from the man who, eight months ago, had leaned out of a car window and shot him dead. It wasn't even as if she'd had the choice: him or me. It had been him *and* me. Or him, period. No one could blame her, no jury would convict her, what she did made perfect sense. It wasn't her fault. And yet, if the situation were reversed, he would have fallen with her. Or caught the bullet in his teeth. He would have done *some*thing. She was sure of that.

She rested her forehead against the chilly window and waited, concentrating on the dog—dirty white, shaggy, long tail with no curl—until it disappeared around the corner of the building. By that time the floor had steadied under her and her head had cleared. She rinsed her mouth with Coke, spat into the wastebasket and then, limping slightly, made her way down the hall to the bathroom.

The shower was full of thousand-leggers. She cleared them out with toilet paper, flushed them down the john and turned the water on as hot as it would go. She stood in the shower for twenty minutes or more, thinking of nothing at all while the scalding stream played across her shoulders and over her left leg, reddening the scars. When the water began to cool she toweled herself dry. She combed her hair and brushed her teeth, all her movements brisk, economical, automatic. Her mind stayed empty. The ache in her knee had eased.

The drink machine hummed softly in the quiet hall. A board creaked under her weight. One of the bare forty-watt overhead bulbs flickered nervously as she passed, damp towel slung over her shoulder. And then, from behind one of the doors, a woman's voice cried hoarsely, "Aah!" Just once. Nothing else. The girl closed her own door gently and leaned against it. She had just remembered who it was that the red-haired black man at the bus station reminded her of.

Ginger Holmes, a horseshoer at the Charles Town tracks, was a man well into his forties—a good deal older than Chance, but the two of them had been friends. Sometimes in the evenings they'd play cards, sitting in Ginger's kitchen with Ginger's wife Delois washing dishes at the sink and his dogs asleep under the table and his kids glued to the TV until all hours. Five-card stud, nothing wild; Chance dealt like there was no tomorrow. Laughing, his head thrown back, "Ain't life a crazy crapshoot!" He'd one-hand the deck, shucking the grimy blue bicycle cards off the top and snapping them across the table with his thumb and forefinger. But Ginger . . . Life was no crapshoot and poker was no game. There were rules to follow, odds to figure, steps a smart man could take. When Ginger dealt he peeled the cards carefully from the deck and tweaked them to be sure there weren't two stuck together before he set them gently down.

They were a pair, all right, like the Odd Couple on TV, almost. Ellen used to laugh sometimes, watching them, and wonder how two guys so different could get along so well. Chance—even his name gave you an idea of what he was like. Life was a game, a gamble; if you won you bought rounds for your friends or you kept on playing until you lost and your money ran out. And when you lost, well hell, sugar, tomorrow's nothin' but another day. He was fun to be with, exciting; no way you'd ever be bored with him around. But Ellen had known—forever, it seemed—that life was no game; it was a narrow, twisting path, dark and dangerous and subject to change without warning. And if you wandered, if you took even a single false step, you could fall.

Chance just laughed when she tried to explain it. "So you fall a few times," he said. "So what? Everybody falls." All it meant was that you bounced back up again. "Your luck changes, or you work some kind of deal. Hell, sugar, I done it a thousand times myself." She couldn't seem to make him understand that it didn't work that way; that you didn't necessarily just fall down, you could fall *in*. And what you fell into wasn't something you could just bounce or even climb up out of. It held you powerless, whatever it was; sucked you down like quicksand and closed over your head. Swallowed you—so much for your luck, your deals; you might as well never have been. So your only hope was to stick to the path and move slowly, testing the ground every step of the way before you trusted it with your full weight.

Chance didn't understand this at all, but Ginger did, or seemed to, in a way. He was a Godfearing man, to begin with, and although he wouldn't have agreed with Ellen that this didn't matter worth a hill of beans, he did seem to know that you couldn't stop there. He had a cross and a paint-by-numbers Jesus that his wife had done, both of these in his living room, and he never missed a Sunday at the Baptist church in Charles Town, but he also had a rabbit's foot, a lucky shamrock (a real one, all the way from Ireland, he said), a lucky hat to wear to the races, another one for poker and another different one for fishing, and he knew you couldn't stop there either. He'd developed certain rituals for dealing cards, for shaking up the dice; glasses and bottles just so on the table, chairs arranged a certain way, if you spoke while he was dealing he'd take back the cards and start all over again. Superstition, Chance called it, but Ellen didn't see it quite that way. Ginger thought things through. He looked before he leaped and covered all the bases, just in case. It couldn't hurt. He had seven kids, which was his lucky number.

"What you gonna do now?" Chance joked when Bubba, the youngest, was born. "Sleep on the roof?"

Let him laugh, Ellen told herself. She loved Chance, but Ginger had the right idea. He was careful, Godfearing; he looked before he leaped, and all things considered he was the last person on earth that she would ever have expected to cut another man's throat in a knife fight in some bar.

No way, she'd insisted. "I *know* Ginger. It must have been some other guy."

Chance shook his head. "We're all of us killers, sugar. It's in us when we're born." It was the liquor acting in him, Chance said. And later, "That dude said things to Ginger a man just can't ignore." And later still he said, "It all comes down to how far you'll let them push you, sugar. To where you draw the line."

"Where's your line?"

Winter, already dark, the wind rising and cold. But inside, where Chance is working, it's warm, the air pungent with oil and hot metal, rubber and gasoline. Ellen has just finished sweeping up out front, propping up the FOR SALE sign that keeps falling down in front of Mr. Monroe's '74 Dodge Dart. She stands in the doorway of the Quonset hut, watching him. Studying him, really. Chance, short for Chauncey, Griffin. A little short quick wiry guy, a tad soft in the waist these days, up to his elbows in somebody's old Camaro. He's twenty-six but looks older; the life he's led has lined his face and leached the color from his hair. Blue eyes from his Irish father, flat broad cheekbones from his mother's side. Paiute blood;

he swears it's true, despite the hair and the ruddy skin that never browns no matter how much time he spends in the sun. His fingers are stained black with grease, and rain or shine he wears an old red windbreaker, faded across the shoulders to the color of weathered brick. Ellen has sewn his name for him, in rambling white stitches, over the heart.

"Where's your line?" she asks again.

He wipes his hands on an oily red bandanna and puts his arms around her. "Like this," he says. "I draw my line like this, in a circle right around you and me. I got that much, sugar, then they can have the rest."

Back in her room, the girl untied the cord that held the suitcase and began methodically to unpack. She hung her shirts—two faded blue cotton, one green plaid flannel—in the closet beside the vinyl jacket and the yellow nylon blouse that went with the orange jeans. She put the jeans over a hanger too, smoothing the wrinkles as best she could. Levi's and a turtleneck in one dresser drawer, underwear and socks in another, sneakers lined up beside the needle-heeled boots just inside the closet door. She'd always been neat; she'd learned it as a kid and kept the shop and the garage so you could eat off the floor, Chance said, and the old Airstream trailer where they'd lived. . . . "Sugar, relax," he'd say. "Leave it till tomorrow." She never could make him understand that she had to know where everything was; that the one thing she'd learned for sure in all her life before she met him was that if you couldn't find something, lay your hand right on it in the dark, you had no way of knowing it hadn't been stolen from you, or that it hadn't packed up on its own and gone.

She spent a long time over the dresser top, arranging and rearranging her comb and brush and the lipsticks and eye shadow she'd bought at the Woolco, and the gunk that was supposed to restore her hair to its real color when and if that time ever came. She set out all the tubes and bottles of make-up, the taller ones behind the short ones, with the spaces between them absolutely even. It took a long time but finally she was satisfied. She sat down on the bed, then, and slipped the gun and the baggie with its six cartridges from their place in the box of maxipads.

The gun was a forty-four-caliber Smith and Wesson revolver, old and ill-used, with a quarter-inch of slop in the trigger action, rust streaks on the barrel, its butt wrapped with black tape. The girl hefted it on her palm. It was too heavy for her, a man's weapon, but that didn't matter. She could use two hands. She could rest the barrel on a tabletop or on the arm of a chair. When the time came, she'd figure a way to do what she'd come to do.

Still holding the revolver, she spread the red windbreaker across the pillow and lay down with her face beside it, shutting everything out of her mind but the faint sweat-grease-whiskey smell of the coarse red cloth and the feel of the black tape warming in her hand. Chance? she said, and waited, listening, making herself empty, but there was nothing to hear but her own breathing and the rain.

3

SHE SLEPT until six thirty. When she got up the rain had quit
and the sky had the cold no-color glare of sheet ice. She opened
her window and leaned out. Cresta, Nevada. A wide-open
place, he'd said, and so she had reasoned that one more brassy
blond cocktail waitress shouldn't attract too much attention.
But Cresta didn't look wide open, particularly. It could have
been any town anywhere—any one of twenty or thirty little
towns where she and Chance had stayed, near this cycle park
or that fairground or some dragstrip or other. It could almost
have been Scott's Run, West Virginia, where the two of them
had lived for more than two years in the old Airstream trailer
beside the Quonset hut he'd leased on the edge of town. Custom
Engine Work. Lawnmower Repair, Used Cars and Bikes For
Sale. She'd wanted to cross out Bikes and put Motorcycles,
but he said no. Anyone who didn't know what a bike was, he
didn't want anything to do with them.

Not the wild town she'd imagined, then, but half-familiar,
homey. It wouldn't have surprised her to see someone she
knew. It almost wouldn't have surprised her to see Chance
himself, walking along with that cocky stride of his, waving
and calling to all of his friends. But the only living soul anywhere
in view was a kid with bushy sideburns who broomed grease-

sweep around in circles on the concrete apron in front of the pumps at the corner Texaco and wagged his behind to the disco blaring from his portable tape player. And aside from Millie's and the gas station, all she could see was a drugstore, a hardware, a realty and two bars.

The girl—not Helen Flynn but Ellen Flint—leaned farther out her window, looking up and down the street. The air was clear and wintry; the sky had begun to change from ice color to blue. Frost lay in patches on the roofs of parked cars and on windows across the street where the sun hadn't hit. The kid at the Texaco finished sweeping and carried his broom into the garage. A paperboy rode slowly by on a blue bike, jacket collar turned up against the morning chill, and a station wagon coasted to a stop at the curb. A woman got out. White shoes and stockings under a gray coat. A nurse, the girl decided. Nurse or waitress, one or the other. The woman crossed the street quickly, her breath pluming behind her, and vanished from sight.

Dressed in Levi's and her sweater, yellow hair tucked up under a navy watch cap, the girl walked quietly down the hall to the red-lit exit sign. She climbed the stairs and sure enough, there was a door out to the roof.

The four-story Aberdeen was the tallest building anywhere around. To the east the town petered out quickly: crooked streets, little houses, a few shacks, then nothing but mile upon mile of high desert and scrub, split down the middle by a highway and rolling away into the sunrise. A dozen or so Herefords grazed in the distance near a line of tall slim trees that grew beside a creek. As she looked, the cows suddenly spooked and took off with their tails up over their backs, stiff as frozen ropes. A moment later a hunter in a vivid orange vest came out of the trees trailing his shotgun by the barrel.

The railroad no longer ran through Cresta. There'd been a cave-in, Chance had said; unstable ground, an earthquake, she didn't really remember the details. But she could see it off to the south, where its bed had been cut into the side slope of a hill.

To the west, Route 212, a good-sized road, wound toward the mountains. The Sierras—tall bony peaks that jumped up out of the surrounding foothills as if something had startled them. Shaggy pine forest blackened the mountains' flanks, thick as a pelt at first and then thinning and dwindling until there were just a few stragglers, more like sketches than real trees, and then there was nothing but sharp bare granite against the sky. Nine, ten thousand feet, he'd told her, maybe more, and already there was a lot of snow. Where the sun's rays struck it, it shot back colored sparks, lavender and apple green and gold. Maybe there was always snow, she thought, that high. Probably there was. It was funny that he'd never said.

He'd told her everything else about the place, Lord knows. Sometimes there'd be no stopping him. Mountain streams that ran icy clear, he'd say, even in August; cold thin air that burned your lungs and played tricks on your mind. Good fishing not a stone's throw from your door, and at night sometimes a cat would scream so close by it seemed you ought to be able to reach out and pluck the sound up and hold it in your hand. "There was things I had to do; I had to leave," he told her time and time again. "But sugar, you know I'm goin' back one day."

Going back. Going back. A place to go back to. She thought of the salt marsh, the rank wet iodiny smell when the tide was out; quiet and loneliness, the ground squelching under her feet. Slow-moving water, thick as soup; bubbles rising from the bottom, forming rings on the surface when they broke. Rings within rings, and at the center sometimes not a bubble at all, but the snout of something hidden—some snake or fish, perhaps a giant turtle, or *something dark and nameless!*—coming up for air. Once as she waited in the tall grass for some gulls

to fly within range of her Daisy air rifle, she had heard a
sound, more sigh than splash, in the channel behind her.
Turning, she saw the brackish water swirl and then draw back,
or so it seemed, from . . . from what, she couldn't tell. The
top of a head, it looked like, knobbed and wrinkled, green-
brown as the water. It looked incredibly old, somehow; old
and strange and monstrous, like something left over from di-
nosaur times. Or even earlier! And as she stared, the gun
forgotten in her hands, whatever it was had raised itself a little
higher, water streaming down its warty ancient brow, and
aimed one flat cold eye her way. That eye had regarded her
and dismissed her in an instant; she might as well have been
the stump of a drowned tree. And yet she felt exposed. No,
recognized. The hair stood up on her arms. The eye had blinked
once, a flicker of pale membrane, and then its owner sank
from sight again.

A log, she had told herself. A rotten waterlogged tree trunk
floating just below the surface. Something had caused it to
bob up when it did, just coincidence that she was there, and
the eye could have been a knothole or the head of a big nail.
Of course it could. But it could as easily have been a monster,
or the Devil himself! The salt marsh was like that. It could
trick you. Men had disappeared there; drowned, it was said.
In quicksand. One false step and it would grab you, pull you
under, suck you down and there was no escape. Every so often
she'd be awakened in the night by an unearthly sound that
was neither shriek nor bellow, but an agonized combination
of the two. Sometimes it would go on and on and on, rising
and falling for hours on end. A cow, Mama said. Stuck in the
quicksand and being slowly pulled under. Sometimes men
would try to save the cow; put a rope around its neck and try
to drag it out with a tractor or a Jeep. But if the animal was
in too deep . . . Mama shrugged. Sometimes the men would
shoot it—a quick, sharp bang, then silence. Other times they

wouldn't. The longest Ellen could ever remember its taking a cow to die was eleven hours.

Mama'd have had a fit if she had known that Ellen ever went into the marsh, but it made no nevermind. The marsh was better than the jetty. Few people went there. Too dangerous, everyone said, but Ellen just smiled. It was only dangerous if you didn't know your way around. Only if you got careless. And she knew the marsh at least as well as she knew the floor plan of any of the little apartments where she'd lived with Mama and Jimmy Lee. She knew the boggy spots that swallowed cows, and the solid spots and the deep pools and the channels where the current pulled with a curious insistence against her legs, against her hips and chest as she waded farther from the bank. Sometimes then a kind of craziness would take hold of her and she'd hold her nose, duck her head and float, letting the water take her. And that *was* dangerous. Because where it could take you was into some unfamiliar cove where you didn't know what was beneath you, quicksand or firm ground or a pair of open, waiting jaws. It was fun to turn loose and float like that—indeed, the danger was part of the fun—but she didn't do it often. She knew better than to push her luck. The salt marsh was like anything else. If you stuck to what you knew you'd be okay.

She never told Chance any of this, of course. It was hard to talk about. It would sound a little weird, wouldn't it? "My favorite place is a swamp." What kind of people liked swamps? And anyway, it wasn't that she'd *liked* it, exactly. In the end she'd come to hate it, and with good reason, too. But it had fascinated her and continued to do so, and looking back it seemed to her that there was a lot to be said for growing up surrounded by quicksand. You learned to walk carefully, for one thing, and watch out for snakes. And she knew that a touch, just a tiny touch, of this caution was what Chance needed. All he needed, to get him back on top of the heap again, where he belonged.

But that had been then and this was now; she had a different purpose in mind. Different purpose and different place, not salt marsh but mountain, not quicksand but rock and snow. Lou French's ranch, the Double Deuce, was up there somewhere—house and barns in the foothills and the lodge another thousand feet higher, where Copper Creek formed the boundary between his property and what Chance called government land, the Toyon National Forest. Less than a mile downstream on the government side was the cabin where Chance's half-Indian grandmother had lived. There was a ridge, he had told her, with sort of a bluff or overlook just before you started down into that canyon. You could see the old woman's cabin from there, and the creek and the footbridge that she'd built with her own hands. It was funny, he used to say. To get to the cabin you had to cut through a draw that was part of Lou French's spread. Of course Lou French hadn't owned it then. People called Teixeira owned it. "But it's funny to think about, ain't it, sugar? Funny the way things turn out."

Funny. The way things turn out. If he hadn't tried to go back there, back in December, if he'd just buried his father and come on home instead of trying to visit that cabin—fire trails and deer paths in a rental car! Like a tourist! As if he hadn't lived there half his life! Two foot of snow on the ground, six-foot drifts; of course he got stuck! And had to walk out; had to walk out through that canyon that was part of Lou French's land. Down the mountain to the ranch, pay one of the men to go up there with the tractor and jerk the damn car free. And then hang around, of course he would; friendly guy like him, he'd take a drink or two, check out the barn, have a look at the horses in the field, find any old excuse to tell his tales. "Yeah, I use to work for him too, you know. Rode his racehorses. His number-one boy, yeah, I sure was. Hollypark, Hialeah, all over. Listen, we was friends."

A couple of drinks, shoot the breeze awhile, have a look around. That much for sure. That much was as much a part of him as the color of his eyes. But then what? She'd tried for months to piece it all together. The fairgrounds. He'd always begin there. It was his favorite story, and hers too. "The fairgrounds." She could just see him, jingling his keys, no reason to stay on but not wanting to leave. Not with the Double Deuce ranch hands, a fresh audience, gathered around. "That's where I met old Lou," he'd say; "I guess it's been ten years." But he could still see it, he'd say, see it as clear as if it were just that very morning, a fine cold day with frost on the ground and the barn roofs sparkling in the sun. And the men would all nod. That was the thing about Chance and his stories. He had a gift; he made them seem so real. "Steam rolling up in a cloud off the horses' flanks when they come in off the track," he'd say, and you could see it. Brown horses, gray horses, the riders tall in their stirrups. "Me and my friends," he'd go on. "Up since the crack, mucking stalls, walking hots, shooting rats in the feed shed. Cards, dice and a six-pack, early as it was." That had been his life, he'd told her. His father's life before him, and what he thought·he'd always do.

But then! "Oh sugar, I can still see that van pull in. It's brilliant red, the reddest red that ever could be, and the trim's all silver and the colored guy driving it's got on a uniform like a five-star general. That much brass and stuff. And on the side it says, real fancy, *Lou French Racing, L-T-D*."

And then the van had stopped and *he* had gotten out the passenger's door—Lou French himself, smoking a cigar the color of dollar bills. "Anybody here looking for work?" he'd asked, and he'd looked at Chance and his friends lounging there by the tackroom door. "Sugar, it was Tony Smith and

Bucky Rowe there with me that morning. And Fred Blaise and Little Al Gonzales. And he looks at them, sugar, and he looks at me and he goes, 'You. You're the one I want.' "

Had he told them that story, those Double Deuce hands? More than likely, she thought. It had been his favorite, after all. If only he'd left it at that!

You. You're the one I want.

The girl gazed out past Cresta's little stores and cafes at the bald snowy peaks and chewed her lower lip. Beautiful country, he'd said. Beautiful and unspoiled and so remote that nobody'd set foot on it since the old woman died but Lou French and his buddies on their hunting trips and maybe a lost backpacker or two. It was good to know for sure that they were up there; that Lou French hadn't changed his plans at the last minute and sailed off to Bermuda in his yacht. They were up there, the dispatcher had said so, and she smiled a little as she thought of them making their way through the sparse high-country cover—watching, listening, rifles cradled across their chests.

She wished she were up there too. She needed the time, Lord knows—the three or four days before he'd be down off the mountain. There was so much to be figured out: times and places. There were plans to make and so much yet to learn. But still, as she stood there on the roof of the Aberdeen Hotel, she was taken with a sudden crazy urge to set out after him *right now*, stiff knee and unfamiliar country and all, and bad weather coming on. It was a need, a hunger, so mindless and powerful that for a moment nothing else existed, and she turned, heading blindly for the stairs. She caught herself— *whoa!*—her hand just inches from the doorknob. Don't be crazy, she told herself. Keep it neat. Stick to the plan.

The plan meant the party. A real blowout, Lou French had said. Smiling at her that afternoon in Virginia. "Think you can trust Chance out of your sight for a couple of weeks next fall?" Ten days or so of hunting and then a real blowout afterwards, he told her. "Strictly stag, but I'll keep an eye on him so he doesn't get in any trouble." And everybody would be home in time for Thanksgiving. Turkey with the family.

And meanwhile Chance's fingers were biting into her arm: *Sugar, what'd I tell you? Me and him was friends!*

There were times when she thought that was the worst part, the stone-hard core of it all. It hadn't been enough for Lou French just to kill him. He'd had to play with him first.

Three days, she told herself. Four at the most. Her hair, when she tucked a stray lock back under her cap, felt harsh and dry as the coat of a terrier.

She ate breakfast at a cafe called the Crossroads, three blocks from the hotel. Cornflakes and coffee were what the budget called for, but she sat at the counter in her old jeans and sweater and her blue knit cap, and had two eggs over easy and a side of sausage and hash browns. There was no telling where she'd be, come lunchtime.

The food was good. The girl ate slowly, surveying the other customers from behind the sports page of the Reno *Times*. Plain ordinary people: ranchers complaining about the price of feed, shop owners and store clerks, a couple of linemen from the phone company. She'd seen them drive up in their truck. The plump gray-haired waitress bustled about, wiping tables and refilling coffee cups, chatting and joking with the regulars, who called her Mrs. Lomax. The girl watched her with growing interest. She was just the kind of nice friendly talkative old lady who'd know everything about everybody who'd ever lived within fifty miles of town. She'd have known Chance, of course. Known him and liked him; she'd remember him perfectly. *Why honey, I cheered so loud when he won his first race my throat was sore for a week!*

She'd have known Lou French too, from the old days. Known

him for the bastard he was. *He fooled a lot of people, but he never fooled me. A bad apple, that one. I knew it from the start.*

The girl wished now that she could say the same. She wished she could say yeah, just as soon as he set his evil foot on our place I began to smell a rat. But the truth was, when he had first shown up all she could smell was money.

That had been nine months ago now, a Saturday morning in February. Chance had gone to the hardware store. Ellen, in the small neat office at the rear of the Quonset hut, scowled at the Balance Owing column in her ledger; worse this month than last. His trouble was that he was just too good-hearted, she knew that. Couldn't say no to his friends, was a sucker for any hard-luck story. A feeder of stray dogs and she loved him for it, but they'd never get that dream trip at this rate— Fort Lauderdale and Disney World, a package deal, specially priced. She'd clipped the coupon from a magazine. But first things first, and at the moment she wasn't sure how she was going to pay the rent. When she heard tires on the gravel out front she looked up in exasperation. Really, she was going to have to speak to him about a thing or two.

But it wasn't Chance, home from Scott's Run in the pickup. It was someone in a black and silver Rolls, and she remembered now how glad she had been that it was Joe Tatum's thousand-cc Honda, waiting for a new throttle cable, that was parked there by the door where anyone coming into the shop would see it first of all. Despite its bent forks it was a sharp-looking big bike that ought to make a good impression on the man who was just then stepping out of the passenger's side of that classy big car.

She could tell right away that he was someone important and maybe even famous. He had an angular face, ugly and handsome at the same time: high-bridged nose, long jaw, squint lines in the corners of his eyes. Distinguished was the word.

He was fifty, maybe, with more salt than pepper in his hair; gray slacks, dark blue jacket buttoned with a double row of gold coins that she knew just had to be real. His black boots were made of leather so soft it didn't shine so much as glow. But for all his finery and his razor-cut hair he looked hard and fit, and you could tell by the way he moved that he was used to having people get out of his way.

"Hi," she said. "I'm Ellen. Can I help you?"

His eyes were green, with light brown flecks. His quick gaze poked and probed into all the corners, taking in Hal Dugan's tractor in pieces by the far wall, the Wagner kid's battered VW bug, the three motorcycles leaning on their kickstands. Ellen hoped he was impressed. She hoped he knew that this far outside of town a mechanic had to be pretty good to attract so much work. "Nice to meet you," he said, and smiled at her, stripping off a fur-lined glove to shake her hand. "Is Chance around?"

"He's in town," she said. "He'll be back in a few minutes if you want to wait."

Still smiling, the man shook his head. But he didn't leave. He strolled over to the Honda, squinted at the forks and frowned. Then, indicating the little Yammy dirt bike, "Is that Chance's?" As if somehow he knew that it was, and that the big Honda wasn't.

"He races it," she told him. "Hillclimbs, mostly. That's his too," pointing to the tarp-shrouded Suzuki on the trailer. "That's a five hundred. He runs it at the Speedway and different places."

"Doing any good?"

"Sure!" she said. "He hasn't been at it all that long, but already he's won a bunch." She looked away. Three races were a bunch, weren't they? And there would be lots more; she was sure of that.

The man strolled to the back of the shop. He examined

some of Chance's carvings—a grizzly bear, a foxhound bitch and pups—that were there on the workbench, and looked at the old slide-action Remington on its rack above. "Same old Chance," he said, lifting the rifle down. "He always was a fine shot. When I first knew him he could dot the *i* in a Miller's can with a twenty-two at forty yards or so, without a scope."

"Still can," Ellen said proudly, and then added, "So can I," remembering the time when her life's ambition—her realistic life's ambition—had been to own a twenty-two.

She could no longer recall which of her mother's men had taught her to shoot, but one of them had, and had even given her the Daisy she used to take out into the salt marsh after gulls. Or she'd sit on the jetty with a screwdriver and a can of Three-In-One and a rag; tear the little gun down, clean it, put it back together, over and over again until she could do it blindfolded. Sometimes she had spent entire days like that, disassembling and reassembling the rifle, ignoring the other kids who hung around, ignoring her brother slumped in his wagon. Two years older than she was, and he couldn't even talk, couldn't go to the toilet without help. Eyes closed, she'd loosen screws with deft fingers and dream of cruise ships on the Gulf. White and clean, strung with pretty lights, her father so handsome in his uniform. She knew he'd come for her one day.

Occasionally on a summer evening when Chance was off somewhere she'd take his thirty-thirty out to the meadow behind the Quonset hut. Clover grew high along the fenceline, and there was a fallen pine where she liked to sit while she cleaned the gun, chewing a stalk of ragweed, smelling the hay drying in windrows beyond the creek and thinking of nothing except that she was happy. Sometimes when she was in a certain mood she'd line up beer cans and bottles on the fence and pick them off methodically, one after another. It had been years since she'd shot the Daisy, since she'd shot anything at all, for that matter, but she hadn't lost her touch and sometimes she'd go twenty shots or more without a miss. Or she'd wait in silence flat on her belly in the grass until the rabbits thought she'd gone and came cautiously out of the tall weeds and brambles into the meadow to feed. She'd pick one out, take careful aim, and then hold the animal centered in the rifle's sights, following it as it browsed until her wrists ached from the weight of the gun. She never pulled the trigger, though. Nor did she ever go hunting with Chance and his friends.

It wasn't that he didn't ask her. He did, any number of times after he found out she could shoot. "Come on, sugar, live it up," but she said no, you go. "Have a good time," she always said. "Me, I'll stay here and stay warm and have something for dinner that don't bleed all over my hands."

Just like a girl, Chance said, and she was happy enough to let him think that even if it wasn't the real reason.

The man turned away from the workbench. He lifted a corner of the tarp and looked at the Suzuki. Ellen could tell right away that he'd spotted the welds in the frame. "That's Chance for you," he remarked after a moment. "He always did have more guts than sense. But this thing's just an accident looking for someplace to happen."

"No it's not!" But it was. Chance had said so himself, time and time again. Poor equipment was cramping his style. With a decent bike, look out Kenny Roberts! There was no telling what he could do.

Ellen folded her arms and stared at the man. What was he leading up to? Something, for sure; she could feel it in the quiet air of the Quonset hut. She glanced past him, out the window at his car and at the dim figure of his uniformed chauffeur behind the tinted windshield. Was it possible? Was this the break Chance was always talking about? "Got to get me a sponsor," he'd say; "someone to foot all the bills, buy

me some decent rolling stock." Manna from heaven, pie from
the sky, and why not? he'd ask, rumpling her hair. "Sugar,
it's happened before. I'm a lucky man, I've been lucky all my
life!"

Ellen said, "That's not too bad of a bike, but you ought to
see . . ." The man had turned toward the door and she reached
as if to catch him by the sleeve. "He's got these plans, he
wants to build this dragster, of course it's just on paper at this
point but I could show . . ."

She couldn't bear for him to get away. She had to keep him
talking—listening, anyway—until Chance got back. But the
man smiled again and shook his head. He was late for an
appointment, he said; he'd drop back by another time. "Just
tell Chance his old friend Lou French said hello." And then
he vanished into the Rolls and the driver started the engine
and they went whispering off down the lane.

Lou French, the girl thought now, mopping up egg yolk
with the last of her toast. *Sugar, this is how it was.* She'd heard
the story so many times it was exactly as if she'd been there
herself and seen that big red and silver van come rolling into
the fairgrounds. Out of nowhere. Brilliant red, the reddest
red that ever there was. Silver letters on the side: *Lou French
Racing, L-T-D.*

FACES SWAM above her. Voices, fading and wobbling: "a look
at . . . license . . . mber . . . the car?"

Cops. Behind them, a white blur. Nurse.

Ellen shook her head. Things blossomed: acid-orange pinwheels, the taste of bile; at least it cleared away the haze.
"They couldn't stand it." Her mind seemed okay but her
tongue filled her mouth and her words caught in her teeth.
"Because of him winning all the time." One of the cops wrote
busily in a notebook. "Down in Florida," she told him, "a

bunch of creeps, they set him up." He'd told her that himself, time and time again. He didn't know who, he said, but somebody, and the word had gone out, down there at Gulfstream Park, and the word was that he took bribes, that he threw races: "Sugar, them fuckers even planted a needle in my glovebox." One of Lou French's horses disqualified after a win, and the Racing Commission had come down on him. "Whole damn world came down on me, sugar, you know it ain't right." And it had cost him his jock's license and a fat fine and his job. "He never doped that horse," she told the cops. "Him and Mr. French were friends. You better check it out."

They'd check, they said, but first . . . "Sorry to have to put you through all this, Miss Flint." She stared at them in terror. It was happening again. *I didn't have nothing to do with it! I wasn't even there!* But she got a grip on herself. The past was the past and these guys had a job to do. They were going to find Chance's killer. She would cooperate.

"We were on our way home," she began. "From the Speedway." The old pickup jouncing and rattling on the high-crowned country road, the motorcycles in the truck's bed straining against the tie-downs as Chance shifts into third heading into a bend. Playing A. J. Foyt. "Sugar, one of these days I'd like to drive at Indy." Idiot lights flicker on the dash, the whole truck shudders; Ellen braces her feet hard against the firewall— "Chance! Slow down!"—but he won't slow down; he never will. He just laughs and the truck comes smoothly out of the bend as it always does and the dark empty countryside slips past. Farms, woods, the smooth oily surface of a pond, and no lights anywhere but their own high beams. And there are trophies on the seat beside her! Two of them! She's impressed and pleased, and so is he, although he pretends he doesn't care.

Tin trash, he says. Fake silver, not even plate. He's seen far better in his time; he'll see far better again, he says. But even so. To her, trophies are trophies and these are beautiful. Much classier than that case of Bud he got for being second in the hillclimb last week. And Chance looks pretty classy too—white-blond hair, cottony eyebrows, little cold stump of a half-smoked cigar and all. She can't believe how lucky she is. When he reaches to tune the radio she leans down and kisses his thumb.

The car comes out of nowhere. A side road, maybe. No red light, no siren; not a cop, just someone in a hurry—doing ninety, easy, as he tops the rise behind them, flashing his lights for them to pull over and let him pass. Chance cusses under his breath, "Damn crazy yahoo!" but he eases the pickup toward the shoulder and the car draws up alongside.

An old car. She has time to see that much. Beat-up fender, one door stove in, the roofline's full of ripples—it's been on its head. It's dark blue or green, maybe it's black, it could even be maroon. At night who can tell about colors? There are two men in it. One drives. The other holds a rifle.

The barrel pokes out the window. Like a broomstick, she thinks, like the handle of a mop, and Chance says, "Hey!" not sounding scared so much as just surprised. He hits the brake and then the gas and cranks hard on the wheel. She sees a yellow flash. Chance grabs his face and seems to jump back or jump up—a sudden violent movement—and then, after what seems to be . . . several seconds? Does she actually count, *one-alligator two-alligator*, is that what you do? There is a yellow flash, Chance grabs his face and jumps, and then, after *too long* she feels and hears a powerful roar that seems to come from all around. The pickup slews sideways, headlights sweeping crazily: trees, trees, a red clay bank. She paws for the wheel, his blood—somebody's blood—burning the back of her hand, and she kicks desperately at his foot, still wedged against the gas pedal. And then they are in the brush beside the road, tearing up saplings, ripping out a section of barbwire fence, bucking over rocks and stumps. Chance has flopped over against the door. She can't see his face, just the dark mess above his ear. His right arm dangles, his hand dances loosely between his knees and he isn't making a sound.

This is not happening, she tells herself. And then a drainage ditch jumps out of the night and grabs them by the left front wheel, and they go over.

"It was those creeps." She forced her eyes open, making sure the cops were still there, still listening to her. "It had to be them. See, he was going to make a comeback, work for Mr. French again."

The officers promised they'd check but she of all people knew what a cop's promise was worth. And in fact they seemed more interested in his recent actions. He did a little gambling, didn't he? And the way he ran that business of his—so much on the cuff, so many favors for his friends. Was his bookie on his neck? Cops! She'd forgotten that people could be so dense. So he had a few debts—didn't everyone? And his were nickel and dime. "He just dabbled," she said warily. Cops. She knew the way they worked, and she clutched the sides of her narrow bed as the old fears threatened to surface. "Just dabbled," she said again. "If he was into anything heavy I'd know it," but she looked away, not sure at all that this was true. *Sugar, how'd you like to go on down . . . ?*

The pickup rattles and vibrates; rough road, one tire's out of round, she can feel it thumping and the broken spring sticks up through the upholstery of the seat and pokes her in the butt if she's not careful where she sits. Pal, the little wooden horse Chance carved for her, bounces on its rawhide thong beneath the rearview mirror. "Funny," Chance says. He's tuning the radio again—he loves music, country-western, has it playing night and day, watches the Opry on TV and knows the words to every song. "Funny, ain't it sugar, how things can turn around." The radio sputters; not a single station coming in. No surprise, not out here in the Maryland boonies where 10 p.m. is like the middle of the night. "Here I was, all set to race bikes all my life, just waiting on a sponsor and some decent wheels. But sugar, you know things've been piling up a little bit just lately—one or two deals that could of gone my way just didn't, not through any fault of mine, you know." Not that he's been worried, not even for a minute, it's not his style. "But still, sugar, when you think about it . . ." He grins and cuffs her arm, his eyes very bright in the darkness of the cab. "When you think about it . . . I tell you, sugar, it's gonna be just great down there in Virginia with old Lou."

Working with racehorses again after all these years! The idea really pleases him. Not cars and bikes, not cold unfeeling steel but flesh and blood. "Sugar, it's what I'm good at, what I'm *best* at, I feel like it's what I'm *meant* to do." And it won't be just riding, either, although he has assured Lou French that weight's not a problem, really, he'll still make one-ten, easy, one-oh-six if he skips lunch. But mainly he'll be a trainer, he tells Ellen, which is a very high-class job, and even that's not all. Lou French has bought new property and has plans to expand, to build new barns, install another half-mile training track. Oil money from somewhere; even Lou French can't swing this deal alone, Chance says. "Sugar, he's probably wheeling and dealing with Arabs and sheikhs." It will be, he goes on over the crackle of the radio, the finest breeding and training complex anywhere in the country.

"And he's going to let me buy in. I know he is." Chance's eyes glitter in the darkness. He downshifts again, muscles the pickup through a series of sharp bends, and then says that it will be just like old times again. Only better, he adds, and Ellen nods and moves closer to him, rubbing his shoulders and the back of his neck. He's wearing just a sweatshirt; she wonders where his windbreaker is. A chilly late-March night like this—he'll be stiff tomorrow. He'll have caught a cold and he's hell when he's sick, underfoot in the Airstream all day, drinking beer and watching the soaps. She smiles. Virginia will be just great, she's sure of that. Not that there's anything wrong with Scott's Run either, for that matter. They could work out their problems, maybe get another little loan from the bank. She'd figure something; she'd have enjoyed it, in a way. She's good at that sort of thing. But now it won't be necessary and she can see that he's glad. And anything he wants is fine with her as long as they're together.

The car comes out of nowhere. . . .

"No!" she cried, and struggled to sit up, fighting to free her arm from the nurse's grasp. "No needles! I don't do that stuff no more!" And to the cops, or to the shadows where the cops had been: "Chance never cut any corners but the same corners everybody cuts. Someone just had it in for him, that's all. You find out who, and get them!"

When she woke, in a long green room noisy with TV game shows and the up-from-the-toes cough of someone in the next bed, the policemen were waiting. A short one and a tall one; the short one scribbled in his notebook and the other asked, "What about relatives?"

She was woozy and sick, having trouble remembering her own name or where she was or why, but she knew enough to understand that if she didn't get the fences up *right now* she might not get them up at all. And she was going to need them, as much to keep the pieces of herself together as to keep the dark car, the broomstick, the yellow roar away. Even though it had been a long time since she'd had any real reason to be afraid of cops, she was afraid of these two now, and she clung to her fear, focused on it, put it to use. The first board, the first nail of the first section of fence. Cops. Skin searches, laughter: *shit, just another runaway.* When they'd ship her back to Galveston she'd leave again, and then she'd left for good.

Relatives? Her nostrils flared; she smelled antiseptics and sick people, and then popcorn, Necco wafers, My Sin perfume. The Corte Madera Theater. Jimmy Lee squirming in the seat beside her, picking and picking bits of plush from the threadbare maroon arms. Beyond Jimmy, their mother's long blond hair shines softly. Her face is pale in the nervous darting light. And beyond Mama . . . Joe or Billy, Danny, Ramon, whoever.

"Mama?"

"Shh!" She hasn't been saved yet. Her eyes never leave the screen.

Not *her* relatives. His. Lenore Hensley, old Lenore his grandmother, dead ten years or more. A tiny little woman, wizened up and brown as a raisin—she was the one who'd raised him, really; looked after him when his father was drunk and his brother Sammy off catting around. Old Lenore, she *knew* things, he'd say. Dry twigs didn't snap when she stepped on them; she could glide over rocky hillsides and through dense brush as easy as crossing a dance floor. And she was the one who'd taught him to carve. Taken him down to the bridge below her cabin, put a knife in his hand and shown him how to find the shapes of birds and fish in the soft pine of the handrail.

He had learned well. Chance was a real artist, everybody said. His little wooden horses, his hounds, his rabbits and deer, they all looked so real that you'd think they'd be warm to the touch. Sometimes, watching him at work, his white-blond head bent low, white-blond scraps of pine caught in the fine blond hairs on the backs of his hands, bright-honed edge of his knifeblade glinting in the sun, Ellen had felt almost afraid of him. Not afraid, really, but something not too different from that. She didn't know why, except that she loved him, and it sometimes seemed that she'd never before in all her life known anyone who'd ever actually *made* anything but trouble.

"Chance was a natural," she told the cops. "He could do so

many different things—carve statues, tell stories, fix any engine, ride a motorcycle or a horse." Stunts too, she added. He'd been with the circus for a while, not a circus exactly, but a Wild West show. "He was the star attraction!" she said. "Daredevil Chance and His Flying Horse Pegasus! They were something to see!" but it wasn't Chance she saw when she closed her eyes, it was her mother at the kitchen table, making lists, making lists: *fix breakfast make beds make Ellie go to school take Jimmy to the dr.* Memo pads, the backs of envelopes, brown paper bags that smelled of garlic and comino spice. *Do nails brush teeth sweep under beds;* her purse always full of crumpled paper, the table littered with eraser crumbs. *Cereal for breakfast leave nails for later wash hair not dishes pay the rent.* Not that the lists ever did a bit of good. And why, the girl wondered dimly, was she thinking about her mother, about T-for-trouble Texas now? She'd put all that behind her. He'd done it for her, really. Given her a life. Another board, another nail, too late.

You go, Ellie-lamb. Mama is so pretty. Even when she's pale and jumpy, even with the sullen bruise on her cheek. A natural blonde. A high school graduate. Don't even ask where he's gone. Put Jimmy in his wagon and go see the landlord.

You go. It means that the man has left, Ramon or Danny or whoever, and he won't be back and the rent is due. It means they'll be moving. Ellie doesn't mind, really, and she doesn't care one way or the other about the men—except the ones that hit Mama, of course, and the ones that hit her and the ones that aren't nice to Jimmy Lee. After a while the houses all run together in her mind, into one house that isn't the garden apartment with the view of the Gulf where they're all going to live when her father the cruise-ship captain finally divorces that other woman and marries Mama, his one true love. And the men run together too, after a while, into one man who isn't her father and who isn't nearly good enough for Mama, who is pretty and a high school graduate and has had such rotten luck.

If only I could find a decent job! But she can't, and she won't— shouldn't have to—take just any old thing. Won't wait table, isn't cut out for it, she says, or for checking at the Sav-A-Lot. "A secretary," she tells Ellie, "that's what I'd love to be. Wear pretty clothes, work in a nice office, have lunch with the boss," but it takes extra schooling, typing and dictation, and there's no money for that and no time either. The one time she started a course she dropped out because the teacher was so rude; she shouldn't have to take that kind of crap. She's tried beautician, receptionist, salesgirl at J.C. Penney, but it never works out. "We'll just hold on, lambie, till your daddy comes back, it won't be long."

But meanwhile the rent has come due and the man is gone. *You go, lambie. Take Jimmy. And remember to smile.*

"We want to notify his next of kin," the tall officer said, and the little one's pen scritched as he wrote and the woman in the next bed coughed and coughed and spat into an enameled bedpan. The girl stared in awe at the TV screen where Brother Hosea was praying over her mother and Jimmy Lee.

"Next of kin," she said, and almost giggled with relief. It wasn't Hosea after all, or Mama or Jimmy either. It was just some people, plain ordinary people playing a quiz game. An emcee in a plaid jacket was talking to them. They were from Wisconsin, a husband and wife, they knew the answers, buckaroo was a Spanish word, it meant cowboy, their kids were bright, not like Jimmy at all, and Chance had had no family since his father died last Christmas. No mother since he was a kid; older brother killed in Vietnam. "Chance's feet were flat," she told the cops; "the army wouldn't have him." She was all he'd had and all he'd needed: *you and me, sugar. I got that, then they can have the rest.* But the fences were up now and she felt nothing. Even the cops didn't scare her anymore. She was over eighteen. Independent. They weren't going to send her back to Texas. "His folks are all dead," she told them and then added, "same for me," thinking that it might as well be true—that in a sense she herself had died. Ellen Flint? Who was that? Someone she used to know.

After that it wasn't too bad. Policemen drifted in and out; she answered their questions with cool detachment. "Yeah, he was dead before we rolled. He had to be. I mean, the top of his head was just gone."

Nothing to it. She felt nothing. The fences were up; she'd be okay. Coolly, ignoring the knowing smiles, she explained that she and Chance had been partners. "Business partners. I'm a high school graduate. I'm good with numbers and I can type. I kept the books and all." She knew they didn't really believe that was why he'd named her on his life insurance but she didn't care. The money—a few thousand cash—wouldn't begin to cover the cost of putting her knee back together but she didn't care about that either. And anyway, everyone was saying not to worry, the county would take care of her.

She was willing to let it. Or not, as it wished. Either way, it was all the same to her.

Days passed. A week, and the only news was that there was no news. The cops were still checking leads, couldn't rustle up a soul who'd known him down in Florida, couldn't even find the bullet that had killed him. Must've gone out through the windshield, they seemed to think; the angle would have been about right.

Chance shot dead and her with four cracked ribs and a knee patched together with chewing gum and wire and some fancy surgeon's best guess, and the cops were doing all they could, she knew they were. These things took time, some things you just couldn't hurry and what difference did it make? Chance was gone, Ellen was gone; the girl who was left ate and slept and watched TV. And then on the third of April two men went on a tear in Fort Arthur, shooting up streetlights and killing a schoolteacher on her way to the PTA. They were brothers, Amos and Calvin Eustice. They drove a beat-up black Impala with a mashed front fender and Calvin owned a Winchester thirty-aught-six. They swore they'd been at Rehoboth Beach the night Chance was killed, driving around and looking for girls.

"But nobody saw them." Detective Smith, the big cop, was pleased. "Looks like they're the ones!"

Amos and Calvin Eustice. Nineteen and twenty-three years old, poor boys from the red clay country; they were the ones. The girl lay in the dark ward that night, practicing believing she thought they were the ones. They were the ones. There was no other explanation and what did it matter that there was no reason either? She told herself it was good that there was no reason; that she liked it better that way. Better to be struck by lightning, wasn't it? better to be swallowed by the salt marsh, run down by a skidding car; better even to be born, well, *slow*, like Jimmy Lee. Better even that than to be marked, stalked, set up. Anyone could be the victim of chance. Everyone's number came up sooner or later. What the girl didn't want to think about was someone methodically thumbing through the deck. King, queen, jack; discarding, discarding. *You. You're the one I want.*

4

WHEN SHE HAD finished her breakfast she bought a local map
from a vending machine at the Texaco. Towns to the south:
Iron Springs and Boreen. To the north and east: Kirby, Pomo
Valley, Rio Seco, Mathersville. To the west, nothing. Just
mountains, and Route 212 snaking its way toward Littleboy
Pass. Ninety-two hundred feet, the map said. The girl was
impressed. She stood at the corner of Chester and Main, studying
the map and glancing up at the mountain and down at the
map again. Ten miles outside of town, five miles to the inch;
Lou French's place ought to be about *there*, she decided, and
marked an X with her thumbnail near what showed on the
map as a sharp bend in the road. She would have to go there.
Soon. Make her final plans. But meanwhile, there was the
national forest boundary and there was Copper Creek. Her
scalp prickled; she raised her head and looked at the mountains,
breathing the cold clear morning air and listening to the shouts
of some children in a schoolyard somewhere. His school? If
she went there could she find his desk—his name carved on
it all those years ago? There ought to be something. It was
his hometown, after all. A bell rang. The children's shouts
died away. A gasoline truck rumbled past: not Texaco, Shell.

Moving stiffly, favoring her left leg, the girl followed Chester

Avenue past the back of the hotel, made a left at the depot onto Monte Vista and crossed a section of abandoned railroad track. The rails were orange-brown and grainy with rust, the ties rotted through. Earthquake? Landslide? Hands in the pockets of the faded red windbreaker, she walked slowly down Railroad Avenue past the U-Sav Grocery, Bundy's Cards 'n' Gifts, East Slope Properties. Tony's Great Pizza, boarded up. Auto parts, a dry cleaner's, her choice of Standard or Shell. No name she recognized; nothing of him here.

Just outside of town, Monte Vista ended in a T. Right turn for the county landfill and a spectacular view of the mountains; left for the fairgrounds. There was a billboard and a reflector-studded arrow, shot full of holes as a cheese grater, pointing the way. Destruction Derby and Quarter Midgets. The sign jumped right at you, with red cars and orange flames and yellow lightning-bolt letters, but you could see, in places where the paint was scaling off, that there had once been a picture of racehorses. Two miles. Her knee had loosened up. She kept on walking.

The barns were gone. She'd known they would be; the track had been closed down for years, ever since Arroyo Park had opened, forty miles to the southeast. But a number of trainers had stayed on there for a while, using the barns and keeping the track up themselves, more or less. It was cheaper than Arroyo, Chance had said; cheaper by a mile, and an easy van ride over and back on race days. A lot of people he knew had done that, he told her. "Sugar, didn't nobody from there really make it big but me."

But then the barns had burned. No serious injuries, but a lot of uninsured feed and equipment had been destroyed. Much of what was left had been auctioned off and the men, Chance's friends, had drifted on to other tracks or other jobs or had simply disappeared. He'd shrugged. "Guess it just didn't seem worth it to nobody to build the barns back up again, but, sugar, you know it's a shame. When I was down in Florida, going good, I use to think about it sometimes; think about how one day I'd take my kid there. Show him where his old man got his start."

And Ellen had laughed "What kid?" Just joking. She hadn't meant to make him mad.

The fairgrounds looked more prosperous than she had expected. There were exhibition buildings and livestock pens, and a rodeo arena with lights and an announcer's stand. The bleachers had been recently painted red, white and blue, and looked bright and clean with the sunshine on them. The girl climbed up to the top row of seats for a look at the track and the muddy infield. Even though she had seen hundreds of races at Charles Town, it was hard for her to imagine clearly this part of Chance's life. She had grown so used to the bikes, and yet, when she first met him he had still been training horses. Not for racing, though, for Harvey Cloud's Wild West Rodeo Troupe.

The first time she'd ever seen him, in that dusty field near Murphy, Oklahoma, he was down behind the makeshift stock pens with a bunch of his buddies, trying to sucker some city-looking bozo out of twenty dollars. Chance held a scrawny little brown horse by the bridle. A short distance away stood a yellow Ford Fairlane convertible. "Twenty bucks says ol' Peggy here'll jump right on over that car," Chance said. Of course, she didn't know who he was yet, but she could tell he was really someone: small and neatly built, his hair bleached almost white; he wore a white shirt and almost-white blue jeans, and the sunlight seemed to pick him out and touch him in a special way.

The rodeo was over. Most of the acts had moved on to the next town and there wasn't much left but some torn-up ground where the arena had been, a local crew dismantling the bleachers, and the dozen or so horses and steers still in the stock pens because the truck that was supposed to carry them had broken down.

The convertible wasn't Chance's, it was Harvey Cloud's, but Chance used it in his act, and unless Harvey's girlfriend wanted it Chance usually got to drive it from one town to the next. A piece of shit, he called it, nothing like the red Buick Riviera he'd had when he was really going good down there in Florida. That Buick had had real-leather upholstery, he said. It had racing slicks, a stereo tape deck with rear speakers, cruise control, a CB, a Fuzzbuster; everything, he said, but retractible landing gear. Now sugar, *that* was a car! The Ford Fairlane had a burned valve and a hole in its radiator the size of your fist. All it was good for was a horse hurdle, he told her, but it was plenty good for that, and Daredevil Chance and His Flying Horse Pegasus were one of the best acts Harvey Cloud had ever had.

Ellen didn't know that then, of course. She'd never heard of Harvey Cloud's Wild West Rodeo Troupe, and Murphy, Oklahoma, was just someplace she'd ended up—only a year since she'd left Galveston for good, but it might as well be fifty the way she felt. She'd covered so many miles, swallowed so many pills, smoked so much weed; one place was just exactly like another, it seemed to her, except that some were worse. She didn't know Daredevil Chance Griffin from a hole in the ground and couldn't care less, just resting in the shade of a tree, holding onto the trunk while she waited for whatever that trucker'd given her to wear off so Hosea would quit telling her to pray and Mama'd quit looking at her out of every window she passed. Car windows, bus windows, the front windows of stores: *Lambie, don't you want a miracle?* As if there was any such a thing. Jimmy's face floated before her, eyes blank and mouth wet with drool, to remind her that there wasn't.

The city boy eyed the convertible. "Can't no horse jump

that," he said firmly and the others all laughed. And then Chance had wound his fingers in the horse's bristly mane and vaulted onto its back. No saddle. Ellen had never seen anything like it outside the movies.

"Twenty bucks." He was guiding the horse with just his knees, making it dance this way and that, the reins hanging loose on its neck. "Come on, what you got to lose?"

"Don't want that responsibility," the bozo muttered. "Don't want to see nobody get killt, that's all." But Ellen could see him wavering, looking from the little horse to the big car and back, thinking of easy money. And then the sunlight seemed to gather and darken and focus in on Chance so that he blazed orange for a moment like a torch or fiery sign, and she heard herself say, "Side bet." Her voice seemed to come from somewhere behind her, maybe off to the right a little. Not out of her mouth, for sure. It scared her. She'd been feeling for weeks that parts of her were getting ready to break loose and fly away again, that she was losing control and would end up back in Texas on her knees. On top of that, she was broke. She had no business betting, even on a sure thing, which, to her mind, this definitely wasn't. She kept her jaws clamped shut, back teeth grinding together—pretty soon her head would clear and she'd be on her way—but the words shaped themselves and sprang forth all on their own. "Another twenty says he makes it."

She had been standing in the shadows by the end of the stock pen. Now she moved cautiously out into the hard white dazzle of the August afternoon: a dirty, lank-haired seventeen-year-old, broad-hipped and heavy, acne blooming on her forehead and chin. The men laughed. Hey, look what the cat drug in! But the blond one, Chance, wheeled the little horse left and right just using his knees, and he said to the city boy, "Ain't you man enough to take a lady's bet?"

A lady. It was as if she'd been waiting all her life. *Find out*

what they want, and be it. And that was how it had begun for
her, with a yellow Ford Fairlane instead of a bright red van,
and instead of a rich millionaire a stunt rider with a head full
of schemes. Not Mama's idea of a miracle, perhaps, but good
enough. She'd been struggling for so long, floundering knee-
deep in shifting sand, it seemed, until he reached out to her—
a lady!—and carried her with him as his brown horse launched
itself into the shimmer of heat and dust and sun above the
open car.

Salvation, she thought. No, more than that; much more
than that. She wasn't just saved, she was safe. Out of the salt
marsh, up on solid ground.

Harvey Cloud made it clear that he liked things better when
there weren't any extra girls around. It wasn't like he was
running a pleasure palace, he told Chance, life wasn't just fun
and games. "You're on the payroll, boy." He looked at Ellen,
polishing boots in the meager shade of a small tree, and back
at Chance, who'd been making sketches in a spiral notebook
which he half hid behind his back when he saw Harvey coming.
"I want you working," Harvey said. "I don't want you goofing
off. Not in my Ford Fairlane, no sir."

Ellen knew it had been too good to last. She'd been with
Chance a week, eight days actually, traveling south with him
from Murphy, Oklahoma, almost to Dallas and north again
to Ponca City, where they were now, Friday, in a supermarket
parking lot on the edge of town, getting set up for the evening's
show. She had ridden with him all that way in the Ford
Fairlane convertible and stayed with him in Big Red's Tourist
Cabins and the Lone Pine Motel, the Hilltop Vu (more cabins)
and another place that she never did learn the name of because
the sign was gone. She guessed she couldn't blame Harvey
Cloud for thinking what he thought, but he was wrong. Chance
had respect for her. He kept his hands to himself. He even

turned his back so she could change her clothes in private.
And when it had gotten to be ten thirty that first night back
in Murphy, he had rolled up in a blanket on the floor: "Hope
you don't think I'm a party-poop, but I got to get up at five."
A minute later he was snoring.

That had been a real surprise, and she had been grateful.
And the next night, the same thing, and the night after that
and the night after that, with no change in sight except that
by now she wasn't so much grateful as she was puzzled and,
as the week wore on, disappointed. But she could tell that the
men in the crew all thought she was putting out for Chance,
and there was no real reason why Harvey Cloud should think
any different. And he was the boss. If he told her to leave,
she guessed she'd have to pick up and go.

"I don't care what you do on your own time," Harvey told
Chance. "But you're on my payroll, and the Ford convertible's
my property. I don't want you goofing off on my time or in
my car."

Harvey *said* he was Apache Indian, but Chance had told
her that was a lie; he was Greek or Italian or something, and
didn't have a drop of Indian blood. He was a very fat man,
short-legged for his size, who wore silver-trimmed sombreros
and dark blue business suits, wrinkled and wilted from the
heat. He had long oily black hair tied in a ponytail and he
fluttered his pudgy hands in a womanish way when he talked,
flashing his diamond rings. Ellen thought he must be very
rich. He drove a Cadillac that looked almost new, and he and
his girlfriend always stayed in a nice motel—the kind with air
conditioning and a pool—instead of in the cottages with the
riders and the crew. But Chance said no, he wasn't rich.
Chance knew what rich was, he said, and this wasn't it. Harvey's
rings were fake. He wasn't even getting by, couldn't make
ends meet, he'd be belly-up before the year was out. "Harve

don't have but one class act, sugar," he told her, "and that's me."

And Chance's act was classy, no doubt at all about it. When he put on his white buckskin jacket with the fringe on the sleeves, and his wide white chaps and the silver spurs with the star-shaped rowels, she'd get the strangest feeling in her stomach. Churchy in a way, but in another way not churchy at all, but not dirty either. True love. It had to be, and he still hadn't laid a hand on her. She could hardly bear to look at him because of what she knew was showing on her face.

The crowds loved him too. They'd cheer when he'd gallop into the arena, and then all the talking would stop while the crew positioned the car just so for him. And then an utter and absolute silence would fall while he gathered his reins and wheeled the horse Pegasus around in one last circle before he made his jump, as if the churchy part of what she felt was spreading over everyone. And when he was over safely, there'd be a kind of gasp of relief from the crowd and then they'd all cheer some more. You could see on every face how glad they all were that he had made it and was safe.

"Who's goofing off?" Chance took one of the boots that Ellen had polished for him and held it up, turning it this way and that in the hot hazy sunlight. But he wasn't looking at the boot, he was looking at Morna, Harvey's girlfriend, standing there with her hand on Harvey's arm. Morna was an exotic dancer, or had been before she retired, and stood half a head taller than Harvey did. Ellen found this reassuring—she herself was several inches taller than Chance. Taller and heavier, too, although she'd already made up her mind to diet. Morna had a big chest and always wore very revealing clothes, and Chance looked at her and grinned. Then, flicking an imaginary speck of dust from the glossy toe of the boot in his hand, he said, "You got any complaints about the job I'm doing, Harve?"

Harvey said not exactly. Not at the moment. "Just keep it in mind, Chance, that's all. We got to be in Red Cloud by noon Friday. Don't make me come looking for you." He turned as if to leave and then said over his shoulder, "And I don't want to hear anything more about adding on a motorcycle act, either. This here's a Wild West show, not Indianapolis." Before Chance could answer, off he marched on his stubby legs, with Morna striding gracefully beside him.

When they had gone Chance sat back down in the dusty grass beside Ellen and opened his spiral notebook again. The pages were covered with drawings—animals, people, cars, but lately he was into bikes, he said. Motorcycles. He'd had one once, years ago, a Harley-Davidson that he'd beefed up with the idea of maybe racing it a little, but he'd loaned it to a friend and the friend had wrecked it. "Didn't do himself much good neither," he added, and carefully erased a wayward line. And he'd been reading in the paper about some guy who jumped motorcycles instead of horses. Over a dozen cars or more, instead of just one. "I could do that, I bet," he told Ellen. "Sugar, wouldn't that be something?" Old Harve was blind and crazy too, and deserved to go belly-up if he couldn't see the possibilities in an act like that.

Some of Chance's motorcycles were drawn side view, with high-riser handlebars and custom-designed gas tanks painted with flames or stars and stripes painstakingly colored in. Others came at you head on, drawn in such a way that the front wheel seemed almost to have burst free of the page. Chance said this was because of perspective, which had been explained to him by a man he'd met down in Florida: "A portrait artist, sugar. He was famous, and a real good friend of mine." Later that day he took her out to the highway, which was straight and flat, reaching away into the late-summer haze that blurred the line between earth and sky. He made her stand there as the cars and trucks whizzed past—huge and heavy, smelling of diesel fumes and hot rubber—and then dwindled away, losing their shapes in the heat and distance; shrinking down, drawing down to a point like the dot of an *i* and then disappearing altogether. Ellen reached for Chance's hand and held on. She wasn't sure she understood perspective, not in any way that you could draw on a page. But she'd been in those cars and trucks, and she knew now how close she had come.

Bullfrog and fly: *snap!*

They stayed in Ponca City for three days, Friday through Sunday, doing five shows and packing the grandstand every time. Ellen had taken to stuffing an old towel into the hip pocket of her jeans, and when it was time for Chance's act she'd take the towel and give his boots and stirrups and Pegasus's silver-mounted bridle a quick last-minute polish. It still thrilled her, even now after more than a week, to watch his act and to hear the hush fall over the crowd as the brown horse circled the arena and then flew like an arrow straight at the yellow car. Once in a while someone who'd seen her with him would ask her were they friends. Sometimes the way they said it you could tell that "friends" wasn't exactly what they meant. Either way she'd smile and say yeah. Let them think what they liked.

For herself, she didn't know what to think. She'd never known anybody like him. A famous daredevil. An artist. He'd been everywhere, done everything, it seemed—been a carpenter and a mechanic, worked on an oil rig for a while. He told the wildest tales. And he was so polite that he still hadn't laid a hand on her, not even so much as a finger, not even so much as a *look*, even when he was drinking. Which, she had found out soon enough, was quite a bit of the time. It actually had crossed her mind that he might be a queer, but she had watched him carefully for one whole day as he talked and joked with the other men and decided no, that wasn't it.

If it wasn't him it had to be her. She knew she wasn't Miss America—never was and never would be—but he didn't seem to mind. Hadn't he hung around of his own free accord that first afternoon back in Murphy, even after the city boy had paid his debts and slunk away, even after the other men had gone back to their chores? And later he hadn't objected when *she*'d hung around, tagging along while he fed the stock, tagging along when he and the others went across the road to Paula's Diner for their evening meal.

So okay. It was a free country. No reason for him to object if she wanted something to eat. But he'd actually seemed to be glad she was there. He'd offered advice—the meatloaf ain't half bad but the fricassee'll kill ya—and even directed a few of his jokes her way. And when they had eaten and were standing outside the diner and she looked down the highway where the truck lights streamed like ribbons in the gathering dark . . . She had shivered—scared, all of a sudden, and cold despite the heat, trying to find the muscle that would raise her arm and make her thumb stick up. "Sugar," he'd said, "if you got no place else you got to be, why don't you hang around?"

Still, more than a week had passed and he hadn't touched her. He wasn't queer; not a thing wrong with *him*, so that left her. Something she'd done, and Lord knows there'd been plenty. But he didn't seem to mind when she told him she'd dropped out of school, quit going to church, taken some turns when for sure she should have stayed straight. "No angel myself," he said, and it was behind her anyway. She was straight now. No liquor since she'd met him, not even a beer. No cigarettes, no weed. She knew she'd never do drugs again as long as she lived, or look at another man, and this knowledge filled her with a kind of shining joy that was all the better for being kept a secret. It was his doing, and he didn't even know!

She wished she could be a virgin for him, when and if. Men liked to be your first. But if he couldn't be first, for sure he was the last. Even if Harvey made her leave tomorrow, she'd be faithful to Chance Griffin for the rest of her life. She looked at him. It was late at night, some dusty little town. There'd been two shows that day and he was tired. He'd had a shower and a chili dog, and was sitting in the open doorway of their motel room working on a six-pack. Ellen could have had a beer—he'd offered—but Sprite was fine with her now.

Not him, not her, so that left T-for-trouble. It almost seemed that looking into her eyes he must see the rickety little houses, faded pink or yellow, old Hudson pulled up close to the back door in the middle of the night. Cracked sidewalks, gritty dust, the soggy Gulf Coast heat still rising from the pavement at eight thirty in the evening as they head downtown. He could see all that, and hear the dainty tap-tap of Mama's high-heeled sandals, and the squeak of Jimmy's wagon's wheels. Men leaning in doorways; "Hey baby," as they pass.

SO CLEAR: THE dusty street, low stucco buildings, yellow, dirty white; tile roofs, or galvanized; a few chickens scratching in the meager shade of a loblolly pine. The woman is so pretty. She is blond, her skin is pink and white and she knows how to keep it that way. She ignores the Mexican men who call to her as she walks past in her white skirt, her white high-heeled sandals, her red, red blouse, the ornate silver necklace. She ignores the Mexican men and she ignores the women who stare at her darkly and make ugly noises with their mouths as they hang their laundry on the backyard lines. She's been doing laundry too, if they but knew it; he likes to have his things handwashed, his underwear and shirts. And it is such a beautiful day, too nice to hang around the apartment with no one but the baby—and already she's beginning to wonder if there isn't something, well, wrong with him. And now another is on the way. The man will reassure her. Her captain, her wandering sailor, he will laugh away, kiss away, these fears as he has laughed and kissed away her other worries: of course we'll be married. Just as soon as my divorce, live in a garden apartment with a view. And so she is walking the twenty blocks, from the wrong side to the right side of town, with the clothes she has handwashed for him because his wife is ill (his wife is always ill these days), and she ignores the Mexican men and the dark looks of the women. And later she remembers thinking that it was right that it should be such a lovely day, it was right the sun should shine on her because she was in love; she picked some flowers and put them in her hair.

She enters the fine tall building. The elevator makes her stomach dip; it always does. She smiles. Ninth floor. Her white sandals make no sound on the thick carpet in the hall. Still smiling, she knocks on the door—room 932.

Yeah? he calls.

Room service, she tells him. Proud of herself for this cleverness.

Just a minute, he says; she can hear him moving around, muttering and bumping into things as if he's been asleep and can't quite rouse himself. She wants to tell him to hurry. The shirts smell of sunshine; she pictures herself throwing them into the room ahead of her, and him grabbing her and throwing her down upon them, and the two of them doing it there on the floor of the newest hotel in Galveston with the door open in the middle of the day.

The door opens. At your service, sir, she says, and starts to throw the clothes. But then she sees the girl, a black girl, in the bed without a stitch on, legs spraddled. . . . And his face is so close. Little drops of sweat on his forehead and his upper lip. Tail of his shirt hanging out on one side. Buttoned wrong. Another day she'd have straightened that shirt, button by button, kissing each one. (Do you know? she asks. Lambie, do you *know*? Ain't—*isn't* it strange, she asks, oh Ellie ain't it strange when you can be moved just by kissing the buttons of someone's clothes? And then they leave you?)

And there isn't any shame or anything in his eyes. He wants to get back to that girl. Back to fucking her, whoever she is. And *she* is keeping him from it.

The tiniest blue veins in his eyelids.

She says, Here's your laundry, sir.

He takes the shirts and things, smooth and soft and smelling of sunshine.

He says, Thanks.

He closes the door. *Lambie, he closed the door, they'll all close the door if you give them the chance, lambie, are you listening?* If a girl couldn't be pretty she'd better be smart. Find out what they want, and be it.

OF COURSE it might not have happened that way at all. But Ellen believed that it had, that way exactly. And then all those years of hard use and abuse, and then Nashville that time; Hosea saying, Pray! And Mama'd been praying ever since, her looks gone, pretty clothes gone, but never mind. All things considered it was for the best, surely Chance could see that. Because even if Hosea was a liar and a fake—and he surely was!—at least he looked permanent. "And a permanent, stick-around man that tells her what to do is just exactly what my mama needs. She thinks it's God's will," Ellen said, watching Chance closely. "She thinks everything's God's will. Every mistake—it means you're touched by the Devil."

Funny, Chance said. His dad was that way, a little. "Only with him it ain't God, it's booze. He'll tie one on every now and again and mess with some guy's wife. Only it ain't *him*, you know, acting up that way. It's Jim Beam, that horny old goat." He grinned at her wryly and raised his beer can in a kind of half salute. "Lucky me. I got a lot to look forward to."

Not him, not her, not Mama. So that left Jimmy Lee. "One other thing," she said, frowning at a hangnail on her thumb, remembering the deals she'd made or tried to make: *Please, Jesus, if I'm good, if I stay out of trouble one whole week* . . . Hard to do, but she'd managed it once, and nothing. No change in Jimmy Lee at all, or even so much as a postcard from her father. And again, two weeks this time, and still nothing. Except a different man moved in. So no more deals, at least not that kind. But she had looked for signs. *If I hit three gulls in a row*—no, that was too easy. *If the next gull I hit has a black tail* . . . It would fall at her feet, a sign and a blessing, and she would race home with the news.

She had been ten, maybe, or maybe twelve. Already fat, already in trouble at school. No friends. A fight a day. Mama just shook her head; if a girl can't be pretty she better be smart. But all of this could change in an instant, Ellen knew. Their whole entire life would change, they'd be like everybody else. A real family. There'd be no need to fight. And so she had crouched, for hours on end sometimes, half hidden in the hummocky tough grass of the salt marsh, steadying the Daisy with her right elbow snug against her side, waiting for the gulls. One with a black tail, she told herself, until she shot one with an *almost* black tail—dark gray, it should have been good enough!—and nothing. No change. A black wing, then, she told herself, or maybe the whole bird would be black, or else pure white. Something special, anyway. When she saw it she'd know.

And then! Even now, in the motel room in Oklahoma, she could smell the rankness of rotting vegetation at low tide. Not a gull in sight that afternoon, although she could hear them shrieking in the distance. An hour passed, or longer, and the closest thing she saw to a bird of any description was a black and orange butterfly sunning its wings on a dead limb that overhung the channel. She had been about to give up and go home when a gull finally came into view. It was high overhead, far beyond the range of an air gun, but she scrambled eagerly to her feet, pumping the Daisy with quick, practiced strokes. She took aim as the bird wheeled and hovered, so high above her that she could barely make out the cross-shape of body, tail and wings. She steadied the gun—somehow she knew that *this was it!*—holding her breath until the bird centered itself in her sights and seemed to wait. And then she fired. And the gull dropped like a stone out of the sky. No, not a stone, a messy package coming undone as it tumbled, growing larger and larger, wings loose and floppy, not a gull at all but a buzzard—a bird of death! It dropped almost at her feet with a heavy, wet and final-sounding smack and she stared at it in terror. This was no sign! Or maybe it was! She didn't want to know. Hastily she dug a shallow hole, rolled the heavy bird into it and covered it up. And then, her heart still banging against her ribs, she splashed into the brackish water of the channel, up to her knees, up to her waist, and flung the Daisy as far as she could and watched it sink from sight.

That night she made one final deal, for whatever little bit it might be worth: *Please, Jesus, I'll never shoot anything again. Just don't let there be any meaning to what happened.* The next morning she woke up scared, but Mama and Jimmy both seemed okay, and days went by and then a week and nothing happened. By then, she figured, they were safe. Even if a truck were to run them down tomorrow, it wouldn't be because of anything she'd done.

She felt a little silly, having been so worried. All the same, she was glad to be rid of the Daisy. She was through with killing things.

No way she was going to tell Chance, or anyone, about all that. But she wanted him to know about Jimmy Lee. "I got a brother," she said. "He's not quite right," tapping the side of her head with a forefinger. "What I mean, he's slow," and she went on to explain. When she was through Chance said he'd never known anybody that was retarded. "Though," with a smile, thumbing up the tab on another can of beer, "lotta people around this freak show of Harvey's sure act like it, don't they?"

That was all he said. But later, before they went to sleep, he kissed her good night.

From Ponca City they drove east to Red Cloud and from there north again toward a place called Entwistle, Kansas, where Chance said they had a race track for motorcycles and quarter-midget cars. Maybe they could stop off for an hour. "I sure do love bikes," he told her, "and I sure am sick of horses. Sick of the smell of 'em, sick of cleaning up their shit. If there's a dumber animal on God's green earth I don't know what it is. *Damn* Harvey!" he went on, and thumped the Fairlane's steering wheel with his fist. "What's wrong with having motorcycles in a Wild West show? Make it more modern, appeal it to a younger crowd. Hell, sugar, I'd weld me up some handlebars shaped like steer horns if I thought it would make a difference."

It was disappointing to find that the motorcycle track was no longer in business. A riding academy had taken its place.

They left Entwistle early on a Monday, driving hard all morning and into the afternoon, heading for Colorado and trying to stay ahead of a storm coming up from the Panhandle. The air was heavy. Tall purple clouds had stacked up on the horizon to the south, ready to topple, and every so often sheet lightning would flare and there would be a low growl of thunder. Chance had bought two six-packs of Miller's and he kept a can open on the seat beside him as he drove, balanced against his thigh.

The land around Entwistle was flat and featureless—row crops and grain broken by an occasional stream or building or town—and it continued that way for a good many miles before it began to rise and hump up into little hills and then bigger hills dotted with outcroppings of gray-brown rock. There was almost no traffic on the interstate. Chance kept the Ford at a steady seventy-five, pulling at his beer from time to time; Kenny Rogers on the radio, left arm out the window, beating time on the car door with his open hand. He didn't want to stop for lunch. "Storm'll catch us, sugar."

"So what?" Ellen wouldn't drink the beer, and she was hungry.

Chance laughed. "Top won't go up. This pile of shit of Harvey's; a heavy rain'll drown us. I got to keep the hammer down."

By three o'clock the sky was black above them. Lightning sizzled and the first drops of rain struck the windshield. Hole-up time, Chance said. Nothing to do but get off the interstate, find some nice little comfortable roadhouse somewhere and have a few while they waited for the storm to pass.

The next freeway exit led them onto a narrow blacktop that wound through rugged hills toward a town called Skipjack, seven miles away. It was pretty country, Ellen thought, even with the storm gathering. Maybe pretty wasn't the word, but it was different from Texas, and for sure it was different from Oklahoma and Mississippi, Tennessee, all the various other places she'd been in the past year, and she liked the look of it. She liked the fact that she was seeing it with Chance, and although she was surprised she wasn't the least bit sorry when he pulled into a little turnout beside the road and stopped the car.

They were at the top of a hill that overlooked a broad valley with low mountains to the southwest almost hidden by a wall of rain. Beyond those mountains the real mountains began, Chance told her. The high country, the Rockies. And beyond the Rockies were more mountains, the Sierras, not quite so high but high enough. "Sugar, it's so fine out there. Nevada, that's my home," he said. " I'd like to take you there one day."

Ellen didn't trust herself to speak so she just nodded, watching the storm. You could actually see it advancing in a line across the valley; wind bending the trees down, and the dark rain at its heels. She waited, wondering if he would say anything more. The wind gusted, flagged, picked up again and held. Lightning danced and the whole valley was black with rain. Chance said, "I wasn't always with the circus, you know. Wasn't always a damn sideshow act, a damn freak. I use to be a jockey. Thoroughbred horses, sugar, I worked for this real rich millionaire and I was doing so good down there in Florida."

But Nevada was even better, Chance said. "Sometimes I wish I never left. Wish I'd of stayed up there on the mountain, been a cat skinner or a hunting guide."

"Well, why didn't you?" she asked, and that was the first time he told her how Lou French had come to the Cresta fairgrounds in his bright red van. Pointing his finger: *You!*

Racehorses! A jockey! A rich man for a friend! Ellen could only shake her head in amazement: what next? And then when she heard the rest of the story she was filled with anger. How could people be so low? "Just jealous, sugar," he said. "Some people, they hate it when you come too far too fast."

She wished she could have seen him. He'd have looked so fine in those silk suits that jockeys wore. But his scrapbook had been lost. He didn't have a single photograph, not one left out of the hundreds he'd been keeping. "Wish you could of seen 'em, sugar. Me in the winner's circle, getting kissed by pretty girls. Me and Lou, some of the places we went, nightclubs and fancy restaurants and all, and clippings from the papers. Listen, sugar, I was *good*."

She knew he was. Without even trying he was good at

everything, it seemed. A natural. And even without a single photo she had no trouble picturing how he must have looked in his silk shirts and his boots handmade to measure. Same bootmaker Lou French used, he told her, holding up his hand with two fingers pressed together: "Sugar, me and him was just like that." He drank the same whiskey Lou French drank, too, in those days. The good stuff, none of your Ten High, sure as hell none of your Ripple or T-Bird; he could take the beer or leave it alone. And he ran with the prettiest women and drove that red Buick Riviera with the racing slicks on the rear and the black real-leather seats. "Yeah, sugar, I was going pretty good," he said. Nevada fairgrounds to Bay Meadows to Gulfstream Park. One win after another. Then, bitterly, "But they set me up, and then they set me down."

The storm hit them then—cold drops the size of pancakes that exploded on the hood of the car. "I ain't going to stay with this sideshow much longer." Chance's hair was soaked flat to his head and water slid down his face like tears. He leaned toward Ellen. "I ain't going to nickel-and-dime forever. I've been to the top, sugar; I know what it's like to have respect. I swear, I'm going to get it back again."

Lightning struck a tree not fifty yards from where they sat. Dazzling white light, a hiss, a thunderclap; bark, branches and wet leaves showered all around. The air was sharp with ozone. And she could see nothing but his face. She might as well be standing in a pitch-black room with just one window. There's nothing else, she told herself. Nothing but what I can see. Nothing before him, nothing beyond. She took his face between her hands and kissed him on the mouth and then finally—*finally!*—they made love there in Harvey Cloud's open convertible Ford Fairlane, with lightning jumping all around them.

Afterwards he was embarrassed, sitting up suddenly and raking his fingers through his sopping hair. "Christ. Just don't *see* what old Harvey's got against a bike!" And he was sorry too, at least at first; sorry and worried because he didn't have a rubber and he didn't want . . . But it was okay. She smiled, buttoning his shirt, buttoning her own. Nothing wrong with either of them, he was just shy and she liked that about him, and she liked it that he was worried about getting her pregnant. It made her feel good to put his mind at ease. She'd just had her period; she ought to be okay. And that evening when the Fairlane threw a rod and quit outside of Crestfield and the tow truck driver turned out to have a brother in West Virginia who ran a garage and raced dirt bikes on the side and maybe could use a good mechanic. . . .

"What d'you think?" Chance kept his arm around her even when he was talking to the tow truck driver. She bent her knees a little so their faces would be even. "Sounds good." And it did. It sounded fine. And within a week they were in Charles Town, doing so well that six months later Chance leased the Airstream and Quonset hut in Scott's Run and branched out on his own.

A damp chilly wind, smelling of snow, swept down from the mountains and swirled through the grandstand where the girl was sitting. "I'm going to take care of it," she said aloud, "don't worry," and then she reddened and looked quickly around. But of course there was no one to hear. After a moment she stood up and made her way stiffly down out of the stand. She passed up the Poultry Arcade and Mineral Hall, looking for something that would show her where the barns had been. At last, out in a weed-choked parking lot, she discovered some chunks of concrete that might have been foundations, and a few splintered boards sticking up out of the matted brown grass. She kicked at a broken cinderblock, stooped to examine a length of rusty tailpipe. Beer bottles, candy wrappers—she wasn't sure what she'd expected but it wasn't this. A rusty spur, maybe, or a tarnished stirrup; something that would tie him to this place, or it to him, and bring him back to life for her. She took off her gloves, searching by feel through piles of twigs and soggy paper, loosening stones, lifting the slivered corner of a sheet of plywood, on her hands and knees now, breathing hard, digging with a flattened soda can at the cold wet earth.

"THIS WILL BE your room." Angie Vincent's smile looked painted on. "You're welcome to stay as long as you like."

Ray Vincent pointed to a stack of cardboard cartons. He and Angie had cleaned out the Airstream so the new people could move in. "Somebody had to . . ." he began. A big awkward likable man; a hunting buddy of Chance's. Angie was nice too. They were kind, good-hearted people with two cute little boys. A family. They lived near Charles Town, thirty miles from Scott's Run. An extra bedroom. Welcome to stay. Use it as long as she'd like. Watch TV and help with the cooking, baby-sit the kids. When the cast came off her leg they'd help her find a job.

The girl was grateful to the Vincents. They were the ones who had stepped in and taken over, arranged about the insurance and so on. Chance's funeral. And so on. Tying up the loose ends. It was Angie who had brought the little wooden horse head to the hospital. All that was left of the proud bronco, Pal. One of the state troopers had found it—broken, one side badly scorched—on the ground near where the pickup burned. Angie had cleaned it up, drilled a hole in it and bought a silver chain so the girl could wear it around her neck.

Kind, good-hearted people, salt of the earth. She was grateful to them, but now she wished they'd leave her alone. Look at them hovering! Like vultures! Stay as long as you like, when the cast comes off we'll help you. As if she needed help. She was fine. The hospital calm had stayed with her. No tears, no hysterics, nothing could touch her, the fences were solid and strong. Ellen Flint? She knew no one by that name.

Ray, smiling anxiously, indicated the stacked boxes. "Some of Chance's stuff. I thought you might want to keep . . ." He cleared his throat. "Maybe this isn't a good time. Maybe it's too soon? I could take them away, put them down cellar for a while."

"Now," she told him. "I'm okay." And she was. She was fine. Perfect. When the Vincents had left the room she opened the first box.

Fine. Perfect. Except that she could barely swallow. She could barely even breathe; her ears rang, her vision blurred, she couldn't feel her hands at all. Clumsily she reached into the box and lifted out a pair of boots, the leather cracked and stiff, dried mud caked to the edges of the soles. Crash helmet starred on one side from a fall. She traced the thready little dark lines radiating out from the shallow dent. No real damage. It was a good Bell helmet. She put it on and fastened the chin strap. Not a bad fit.

The next box was full of old combs and razors, half-used tubes of this and that. Toothpaste, Ben-Gay, Lanacane. Rubbers. He'd used two at a time, for safety; wouldn't have her on the Pill. Nasal mist; something for athlete's foot; a Fleet enema and a handful of rectal suppositories wrapped in foil like Hershey's Kisses, just thrown in loose with everything else. His bowels hadn't been right since that day down in Florida when the red Buick had slipped off the jack and pinned him to the pavement. Some mornings he'd groan and sweat, arms locked across his belly. "Sugar, I got the plumbing of an old old man."

Metamucil, milk of magnesia, Maalox. The girl unwrapped one of the suppositories and held it in her hand, a little waxy cone maybe half an inch high. It began to melt as soon as she closed her fingers around it.

The third box contained the statues he had carved, and his souvenirs. Ashtrays with maps of California, Florida, Kentucky and New York, reminders of every place he ever was. Matchbooks from restaurants, a white Bible from some motel; in Atlantic City he'd had to borrow the three ninety-eight from her to buy the casino beer mug because his wallet had been stolen. And there it was. Brown glass, the handle made of wood, fixed to the glass with strips of metal that had already begun to rust.

Down at the bottom under everything else she found her high school diploma in its gold-colored frame. Silliness, he'd said when she decided she wanted to go back and finish. "Don't you think I can take care of you?" She knew he could and she knew he would, of course, but she *really wanted* the diploma; she only had a year to go, and finally he gave in. "Go on, then, if it means that much," he said, and he said he'd sketch her picture in her cap and gown. But he never did, and when graduation night came he wasn't there to watch. Something had come up at the last minute, he said. And that's all he said. She figured he didn't want to see her walking down the aisle— even the Scott's Run High School auditorium aisle—with some other guy.

His clothes were in the last and largest box. Jeans, plaid shirts, underwear and socks. The red windbreaker, rank with his smell. The girl put it on, but her fingers were numb and she had trouble with the zipper. She picked up a pair of boxer shorts, pressing her face against them. This touched him there, she told herself, and waited for that fact to take on meaning. But she felt nothing. Nothing seemed to register, or to connect with anything else. She frowned, tried to concentrate. The little bedroom in the Airstream was clear in her mind down to the tiniest detail. Moonlight drifting through the window, the radio down low. She saw the bed, the rumpled sheets, saw herself naked and waiting. He'd always go to the john first. She heard the toilet flush; light fanned across the ceiling as he opened the door. His shadow, his silhouette, then nothing.

It couldn't be nothing. It had been everything; why couldn't she remember? She backed off from the scene, came at it a different way, trying to construct him bit by bit. Blue eyes, broad flat cheeks. Paiute blood. Sugar, this is how it was. And she accepted that, she had always accepted that, but now what she wanted was how *he* was.

She pictured a hand, nails stained black with engine oil, fine blond hairs on the back and on the fingers—just a few blond hairs between the first and second knuckles; they caught the light sometimes. And the corner his jaw made below his ear. She pictured that, and the shape of his chin and the ear itself, soft and pink, complicated as the shells she used to pick up on the beach in Texas, and covered with a down or fuzz so pale and soft it was the next thing to invisible. But she knew it was there.

Eyes, cheeks, nose, ears; his smile had shown more gaps than teeth ever since that afternoon at the Speedway when his throttle stuck and he'd had to lay the bike down. White-blond hair, white-blond eyebrows, lashes bleached silver by the sun. What else? Muscular shoulders for a little guy, ropy muscles in his arms, patch of blond hair on the smooth ruddy skin of his chest like the map of some foreign country, she used to say, and it did look like that, a little: a patch of dense tan fur that started in a point at the hollow of his throat, spread out to surround his nipples and then tapered sharply until it was nothing but a light-brown path over that slight softening at his waist, down over his navel gradually spreading again, coarsening and darkening as it disappeared beneath his belt. Exactly like a map, she'd say. Someplace far-off and mysterious.

Just being silly; it was only hair, after all. But he'd lean close with his lips against her cheek—and just for an instant now it seemed she could almost feel the warmth—sugar, believe me, he'd whisper, I'll take you there one day.

But now it was as if he himself had turned into a country. As if he had grown, expanded, overrun his boundaries so that she could no longer see him all at once but had to travel him like a tourist, from the backs of his knees to his hairy thighs bunchy with muscle, down to his calves and ankles which had always struck her as being almost girlishly slim. Soberly she examined his ass, lifted his dick to feel his balls; plucked at the loose skin, tugged tentatively at a stiff curled hair and then moved on. Toenails. Usually chipped and a little discolored. He'd clip them over the sink and drive her crazy, or he wouldn't clip them at all and go through one pair of socks after another, faster than she could darn them. She knew it wasn't right that his toenails should produce a strong and immediate response (*Chance! For godsake!*) when what he liked to call his equipment did not. So she tried again, going back, taking his penis in her hand, waiting. But nothing happened.

Anger over toenail cuttings. The bathroom door swung closed, she heard the toilet flush, but there was a hole where he used to be, a burned-out place, the edges black . . . as if the Eustice brothers were not just killers but robbers and arsonists as well.

She should hate them, of course, and Lord knows she had tried, scowling at the mug shots Detective Smith had shown her and trying to see something other than just a pair of po'-white country boys, slumped and defeated-looking in their ill-fitting clothes. They were the ones. They *were* the ones. Killers, robbers, firebugs. She had stared at their faces and felt nothing at all, just as she felt nothing now.

Moving slowly, frowning in concentration, she spread Chance's clothes out on the Vincents' spare bed: underwear first and on top of that his jeans and a shirt. She stood by the bed for a long time, leaning on her crutches and looking at his things, waiting for . . . she didn't know, couldn't remember or imagine. But something, surely.

He was all she wanted or had ever wanted or ever planned to want, but now her hands were frozen—gray-pink fingers numb as sausage links. It was almost more than she could do to stuff socks into the legs of his jeans and lay a pair of boots on top of the socks. Gloves in the cuffs of his shirt sleeves. She took off his jacket and spread it over the shirt and set the crash helmet on her pillow. Chance. His shirt. His boots, his jeans. His shape and size, even his smell. Carefully she lay down, hoisting her leg in the heavy cast, and fit herself to those clothes, that shape, her arms straight out on the sleeves of the windbreaker, fingers spread wide on the stiff fingers of his old pigskin driving gloves. She lay there without moving, just breathing his scent in and out, and she tried to reach him and make him real again.

Nothing.

Awkwardly, hoisting the heavy cast, she rolled over and stripped off her own clothes, fumbling buttons with thick fingers, yanking at zippers, and when she was naked she threw herself across his things again, cupping her breasts and telling herself, *him! it's him!*

Nothing. She might as well have been holding handfuls of pudding or cheese. She pressed harder and then harder still, digging in with her nails. Still nothing, not even pain. "Oh God," she whispered, and grabbed herself between her legs. One finger, three fingers, nothing. Truly, he was gone. She had been robbed. Burned out, nothing left but a husk, crisp and weightless as the shed skin of a cicada.

But it wasn't the Eustices. She remembered the broomstick, the flash, the awful empty moment before the sound of the shot, and she knew for a certainty that it wasn't the Eustices, who weren't but a couple of poor dumb country boys with a mean streak, without an idea in this world what they were doing that night in Fort Arthur. The one who'd shot Chance had been cool. Methodical. Taking his time; he'd been there before. She was ready to bet her last nickel on that.

She lay there on the Vincents' spare bed for a long time, holding herself, rocking a little, eyes tight shut; thinking, for some reason, of the coloring books she used to swipe from the Lone Star Rexall back in Galveston when she was small. Not coloring books, exactly—Connect-the-Dots. Follow the numbers with your crayon and slowly a picture would pull itself together out of nothing: a puppy, maybe, or a sailboat or a Christmas tree. And she remembered once when the dots were numbered wrong, remembered how she had worked for an hour and got nothing and ended up in tears. The salt marsh, lightning, skidding cars. Everybody's number came up sooner or later, life was a crapshoot, you took what you were dealt, and it was no use arguing with what was going to be. But if those Eustices killed Chance it meant that nothing bore on anything else in anything but a random crazy way. If those Eustices killed Chance it meant Lou French could have chosen some other boy and Chance could have chosen some other girl and no matter how careful you were there was no way to make it through except by luck. They weren't the ones. They couldn't be the ones. Because if they were, you could connect the dots till the cows came home, and all you'd get was lines.

Six months passed. Crutches, then one crutch and then a cane, and when the cast came off in August, physiotherapy in Charles Town twice a week. Her mind stayed empty, her mood calm, but occasionally she'd lock herself in her room at the Vincents' and tear sheets of Kleenex into strips. She rolled the strips into little pills which she arranged in neat rows on her bedside table before she threw them away. Whenever possible she watched TV. Archie Bunker, "Let's Make a Deal," "The Jeffersons," whatever happened to be on. Johnny Carson was good, and so was anything with cops, car chases and lots of shooting. Shows about suicide. All the different ways you could do it. Ropes, guns, rat poison, gas; you could crash your car, you could carry a bomb onto an airplane. All those ways would do the job. And there was a one-eyed man in Charles Town who, she had heard, would sell handguns cheap and easy, no questions asked. Sometimes she'd pretend her finger was the barrel of a pistol and put it in her ear. In her ear or in her mouth, up her nose, to her temple, standing in front of the bathroom mirror wondering how much, if anything, she'd be able to see between the time she pulled the trigger and the time she died.

Often she'd stay up long after Ray and Angie had gone to bed. Old war movies, the kind that never started before 2 a.m. Those and reruns of "The Untouchables" seemed to have the ring of truth. She'd fix some popcorn, open a can of ginger ale, pull the hassock close to the set so she didn't miss a thing. Ray and Angie would stumble from their room blinking and rubbing their eyes. Was she okay? Would she like to talk? Maybe she'd feel better if she got it off her chest.

She supposed she would. She was calm, her mind was empty, but her body gave her trouble. Sometimes she felt she was choking; sometimes she couldn't breathe and her hands would go numb or her face would burn and tingle. Sometimes she'd realize that time had passed, must have passed, and she didn't know how long it had been or what she'd been doing. She might be in the kitchen drying the breakfast dishes at eight o'clock, and then it would be nine thirty and she'd be in front of the tube with the sound and picture going, and no idea how she'd gotten there or whether she was the one who'd turned on the set or if Angie had done it for her.

And lately she'd started seeing Jimmy. Not Chance. Jimmy Lee, her brother. On the tube: cornflake commercials, National

Geographic specials. He watched her from the pages of magazines. No one else noticed. Not the Eustices, he told her, although he'd never learned to speak. Not the Eustices, he said. There's a reason. Find it.

"Why don't we talk," Ray suggested.

"Well, okay." She turned down the sound but couldn't tear her eyes from the screen. Machine guns whispered. Men spun and danced and fell. Yes! she thought. Yes! That's what it's like! Almost what it's like but there's more blood. Not the Eustices, Jimmy said, holding up a can of floor wax while behind him a pretty blond woman mopped her gleaming kitchen. Reluctantly, the girl turned to face Ray and Angie. "What do you want to talk about?"

Almost-silence in the room. Sounds of breathing, the ticking of the kitchen clock; faintly from the TV, the moan of sirens, the scream and *whump!* of mortars as the show resumed. Not the Eustices. Ray and Angie licked their lips. They wanted to talk about the murder, of course. The shooting. The fire. There was a reason. She would find it. "It smelled," the girl said calmly, "just like a Texas barbecue."

More weeks passed. She watched TV. She baby-sat the little Vincent boys, helped with the cooking, got around pretty well without the cane and she felt nothing, not even when she looked at her knee with its lumps and ridges and plum-colored crisscross scars. Her mind was empty. She was calm. Everything was perfectly okay, but then it was October and Ray and Angie began asking if she'd thought at all about a job.

The girl shrugged. High school graduate, fair typist, good with numbers—she figured she could find something once she got around to looking. She could wait tables, check at J. Kress; one job was as good as another. She wasn't her mother, wasn't proud; it didn't matter what she did. Nor did it matter that a gas station attendant not twenty miles from where Chance died remembered seeing a black Impala, two boys in it, pretty

drunk. "We've got our fingers crossed, Miss Flint," Detective
Smith said, but the girl just smiled politely, even after the gas
jockey picked the Eustice brothers out of a lineup without a
moment's hesitation. It didn't mean a thing. Even after they
shrugged their narrow shoulders and confessed—some crazy
story about rolling dice and it had come up three and the
pickup had been the third vehicle to pass them where they
waited with their whiskey and their rifle in the darkness of
the shadows by the road. Even that didn't mean a thing. The
gas jockey was lying. Those Eustices were lying. They weren't
the ones. Jimmy Lee was right. There *was* a reason.

And Lou French would be at his ranch in Nevada in November. Ten days of hunting, a real blowout afterward; that
would be the time and place. That night, instead of watching
television the girl sat in her room with a pencil and a sheet of
paper. She sat there for an hour or more, barely moving, deep
in thought. Then, in her careful hand she wrote:

1. *Buy gun*
2. *Go there*
3. *Do it*

5

SHE RETURNED to the Crossroads at a little before eleven, and
sure enough, Mrs. Lomax was alone, humming to herself and
rearranging the Campbell's Soup display behind the grill. The
girl sat down at the counter and ordered a bowl of chili.

"Weren't you in here this morning?"

The girl nodded. "The food was so good I couldn't stay
away."

Mrs. Lomax laughed. She'd pass the word along to the cook,
she said. "Thought I reckonized you." She set the coffeepot
on its warmer and leaned her hip against the counter next to
the doughnut case. "I hardly ever forget a face. You new
around here?"

"Just passing through." The chili was the best the girl had
tasted since she'd left Texas; fiery enough to bring tears to
her eyes. "I'm on my way to Oregon"—holding up a thumb—
"but I'm not there yet."

"I can see that," Mrs. Lomax said. "How about a doughnut
or a piece of cake?"

"Just coffee, thanks. You know . . ." The girl hesitated,
breathing in deeply. "I think I use to know a guy who lives
in this area somewhere." She spooned sugar into her cup,

stirred it, reached for the half-and-half. "Chance Griffin. Little short guy with real light blond hair. You know him?"

Mrs. Lomax said slowly, "Well, can't say that I do. But then," she added, "I've only been in town here about six months or so. Mr. Lomax and me, we had a business in Carson City, but we were about to lose our lease, you know, so we moved here the middle of last May. Bought Ace Hardware, over on Ashton, and we're doing real well. Got a little ranchette, too, up in the hills a ways, for when we retire." She reached into the bakery case, took out a doughnut and bit into it. Powdered sugar clung to her upper lip. "Fifteen acres; we're going to raise some Appaloosas. Already got two nice colts. But," wiping her mouth with a paper napkin, "meanwhile if you know anybody that needs any buckets or tools or bobwire, you tell 'em to trot on over and see Mr. Lomax, you hear? They needn't even bother with the Feed and Seed. Fred Blaise runs that, and his prices are sky high."

"I'll keep it in mind," the girl promised. She reached for her wallet to give her hands something to do, but her voice stayed even and her face stayed calm. She even managed a yawn; just a plain ordinary kid in jeans and a turtleneck and blue cap, passing through town on her way to somewhere by the thumb. Fred Blaise. Tony and Bucky and Little Al and Fred. Surely there couldn't be two men by that name, could there? Not in a town this size. She was just about to ask for the check when the door swung open and another customer came in.

A cowboy, she thought at first: tall and lanky, mid-twenties, maybe. His hat looked older than he was. A clump of pale brown sticktight burrs clung to the shoulder of his lumber jacket. He and Mrs. Lomax greeted each other like old friends, and Mrs. Lomax told the girl, "If you're looking for someone who's lived in Cresta awhile you ought to talk to Gene, here. He's practically a native son."

"Really?" She looked out the window and saw a green Dodge pickup. On the door in curly letters: *Gene Rumstead, Farrier.*

"Not quite," he said. He was certainly no beauty. His nose had been broken and his cheeks were pitted with old acne scars, but he had a good smile, open and friendly. "I've lived here about ten years. Why?"

"Ever hear of Chance Griffin?"

He shook his head.

"He's a jockey," she said softly. "He use to ride out at the fairgrounds, years ago."

"I guess that *was* years ago." Gene Rumstead smiled at her over his plate of tortillas and beans. "That track closed down, except for a few old diehards, pretty soon after I moved here. My brothers and I used to shoot rats in a sort of shed they had there, for feed and storage. Some of the men would pay us; I think it was fifteen cents for every dozen we killed."

"Chance was real famous," the girl said. "He left the fairgrounds and went to Hollywood Park and a bunch of other big tracks. Did good, too. But I heard maybe he was back here now." She thought for a moment, then added, "He's a real old friend of the family, you know. And since I happened to be passing through I thought I'd look him up if he was around."

Gene chewed a mouthful of beans. "You ought to try the Golden Starlite, over on Main, some evening," he said after a moment. "Ask for Bucky Rowe. He's one of the bartenders, I think he's a part owner too, and he grew up right here in town. I've heard him talk about the fairgrounds. He'd know your friend if anybody would."

"The Golden Starlite!" Mrs. Lomax clasped her hands beneath her chin, her eyes wide and worried. "Why Gene, that's a *dive!*"

The girl couldn't believe her luck: Fred Blaise and now Bucky Rowe. She would have liked to have kept Gene Rumstead talking, just to see what else might pop up on its own, but he had finished his meal and was counting out bills and change. "Another day another dollar," he said cheerfully. "Take care, Mrs. Lomax," and to the girl, "you too." The door banged shut behind him.

Cresta Feed and Seed was a big drafty barn of a building at the end of Paso Robles Street. It was easy enough to find, but Fred Blaise wasn't there. His assistant was out in the back lot, helping a skinny Mexican kid stack bales of alfalfa onto the bed of a stake-side Ford. Chance Griffin? They looked at each other and shrugged. Fred's assistant said he might have heard the name. And no, he didn't expect Fred back very soon, like not until next week some time. "He's gone hunting with Mr. French. It's deer season, you know."

"With Mr. French?"

"Sure." The man stood on tiptoe, checking the truck's cargo. "He always takes a bunch of guys from town."

"From town?"

"Oh, I know." He stepped back from the truck and flipped the tag end of the rope up over the top of the load. "You read in the papers about the congressmen and astronauts, like they're the only people Lou knows. But Fred and some others from around here, he's friends with them too." He picked up a clipboard from the truck's fender. "We got everything?" he asked the kid. "You remember Miz Laslo's egg mash this time? Man, I don't want her on my case again this month."

The girl was disappointed not to be able to talk with Fred, but she didn't let it show. She fooled around Cresta, killing time, looking in store windows, not sure what her next move should be. She felt tired, a little depressed, even a little—a very little—foolish as she walked aimlessly up this street and down that, staring at the Thanksgiving displays, turkeys and Pilgrims and rosy-cheeked families enjoying apple pies. She told herself that this was his town; that she should feel something. But too much time had passed. The town wasn't his anymore, or the fairgrounds either. She paused to study a particularly elaborate display in the window of a department store. A whole family of mannequins were grouped around a table set with gourmet cookware. There were dishes you could cook in and then put right on the table; there were plates and cups and everything matched. Even the children's sweaters, the man's slacks and the plaid of the woman's dress matched those dishes, a rich deep amber. Even the woman's hair was almost that same color. The girl stared greedily at the scene, ignoring her own reflection on the glass. If only Chance hadn't been killed! That was exactly the life she'd wanted for the two of them. For the three or four of them, however many he wanted in his family. Because she'd talked to the doctor—gone there one afternoon; Chance never knew—and it was okay. She didn't have to worry about any baby of hers turning out like Jimmy Lee.

Eventually, finding herself around the corner from the Aberdeen, she returned to her room. It was midafternoon, but the bed was still unmade, the old shirt of Chance's that she used for a nightgown still draped untidily from the knob of the closet door. Sugar, leave it, but she couldn't leave it; if you couldn't find it in the dark, how did you know it was there? She straightened the bed, hung the shirt in the closet beside the orange jeans. And then she took the pistol from its hiding place, loaded it and tried to slip it into the pocket of the red windbreaker. It didn't fit. No matter which way she turned it something stuck out, and its weight pulled the jacket crooked on her shoulders when she put it on. After a moment's consideration she transferred the gun to the patent leather purse. Even though the purse was too dressy to go well with her Levi's and knit cap, she figured probably no one would notice. And even though she knew Lou French and his friends would be up on the mountain, she just didn't want to arrive at the Double Deuce without the gun.

She hitched a ride out Route 212 with a woman in a station wagon full of crates of yowling cats. The cats, which looked and sounded to the girl like any old cats you might see anywhere, were Maltese, the woman said, and some of them were champions. The girl said respectfully, That's nice, and clutched her bulging purse and turned to peer into the crates again. But the cats still looked like plain old cats to her.

The road climbed more and more steeply as it left the town behind and wound its way through mixed forest, hardwood and pine. The girl leaned forward, peering through the windshield, and sure enough, before long she spotted a pair of tall iron gates on her left with a sign above them that showed a pair of playing cards and the name DOUBLE DEUCE. She didn't say a word, though. She rode on with the woman for a mile or more, until she saw the gates to another ranch. Then she asked to be let out. "Friends of mine," she said. "They'll ride me on home later."

She waited until the station wagon was out of sight and then, heavy purse slung over her shoulder, started back downhill toward Lou French's ranch. It was three o'clock by that time, clouding over, the temperature dropping fast. The wind numbed her cheeks, and the Double Deuce, when she finally got there, certainly wasn't much to look at. Not that it was bad. Plain was more the word. For sure it wasn't in the same league with Olympus, his place down in Virginia.

Wire fences instead of stone walls; the buildings—a house, two barns and some sheds—could all have used a coat of paint. Stacks of weathered lumber in the barnyard and a tractor hitched to a manure spreader that was parked in the drive like the family car. Plain old Hereford steers grazed in the pasture next to the road and in one of the corrals were several large black and white hogs. It was a plain ordinary working ranch.

Nothing special about it except that it butted up to all those thousands and thousands of acres of government land. Best hunting in the world. Jackrabbits to six-point bucks, just name your game. What it didn't look like was the kind of place where anybody in their right mind would keep a four-legged gold mine called Sun River.

Funny, he'd said. The way things turn out. Wire fences, six-foot drifts and a million dollars' worth of Thoroughbred broodmare just turned loose in a field. No wonder he'd come back from Nevada last December with things on his mind. Not saying a word to her but she could always tell when he was thinking. Putting two and two together and coming up empty until the very end. But Lou French hadn't known that. All Lou French had known was that Chance had been at the ranch in December. That was enough. Lou French wasn't a man to leave a single thread dangling.

That was why he'd looked Chance up again after all those years. He'd never intended to hire him on again, or to let him go partners when the farm expanded. He just wanted to pump him, and Chance couldn't have made the job any easier if he'd sat down and drawn them all a map. One of the first things he'd said to Lou French that afternoon at Olympus was how glad he was to see Sun River back in civilization—that was actually the word he used—where she belonged.

They had just finished what Lou French called the grand tour, a ride around the grounds in a pretty little basketwork cart pulled by a pretty little spotted pony. Four barns, neat and white as sugar cubes, one of them outfitted as a veterinary clinic, encircled by the training track. The poplar woods beyond the creek had been the site of the Civil War battle of . . . the girl could no longer remember. Some famous fight. And the house had been built in Revolutionary times. There was no electricity in it, Lou French said, except in the kitchen, for the convenience of the chefs. There had been electricity in the other rooms, he explained, but when he bought the place he'd had it taken out. Just candles for light, the way there had been when the house was new. "Except in the kitchen." He smiled at her; being really nice, she thought. Not at all the stuffed shirt she'd imagined. "How about it, Ellen, do you like to cook?"

Chance hadn't had much to say up to then. Too nervous, she supposed; he wanted the job so bad. She was nervous too, but *somebody* had to talk so she had asked questions, one after another and some of them pretty dumb-sounding. But Lou French didn't seem to notice, even when she slipped once and asked what something had cost; even when she slipped a second time, forgot that she'd already asked him something and asked the same question over again. He just smiled and answered, and once when she said something funny, he laughed. He really did seem to like her, and she looked at Chance to see if he had noticed. But Chance was staring at some horses sunning on a hill behind the barns. Broodmares. Most of them had foals.

"That's my future," Lou French said, looking at the horses too. "My wife swears I think more of those mares than I do of her." He laughed again and winked at Chance, and Ellen laughed and winked back because Chance was still staring, saying nothing, as if the cat had his tongue. He'd never get the job that way! It wasn't until one of the grooms had come and taken the pony and cart away that Chance finally cleared his throat and said, like a speech that he'd rehearsed, "Sure did take me by surprise, Lou, to see old Sunny out there in Nevada. None of my business, of course, but it had me worried." He paused, in case Lou French wanted to say anything, but Lou French was leaning on the fence watching the horses. "Sure is a relief to me to see the old girl back in civilization where she belongs," Chance said, and gave a little laugh. He *was* nervous. Pie from the sky, not just riding but the opportunity to buy in, get a piece of the action. Old times, only better, as he'd said; a chance for the big bucks. He was afraid he'd blow it. Up at the crack that morning, two or three for the road. Maybe it was five or six; past a certain point it didn't matter. Ellen had been nervous too—what to wear, what to say? She had driven the truck while he sang along with the radio, Waylon Jennings and Crystal Gayle, all the way from Scott's Run to Pineford, just north of Richmond, a six-and-a-half-hour drive. Chance had sobered up in a split second, just as soon as they turned in through the gates of Olympus Farm.

Yes indeed, he said, it sure was a relief to see that mare come in from the boonies. Lou French kept his eyes on the yearling colts but after a minute or so he asked what made Chance so sure it had been Sun River he'd seen at the ranch. "If I recall," he said, "there's two or three chestnut mares out there and they all look pretty much alike."

Chance shrugged. He guessed he could tell one horse from another.

Suppose, Lou French continued, "just suppose I was to tell you that Sunny's been here all along. Out in that field," he said, "not even earning her keep last year. She was bred to Gallo Russo but she slipped the foal in July."

Chance shrugged again. He was watching the yearlings too, and it seemed to relax him. "I don't want to argue, Lou. Wasn't but one chestnut mare that I saw, and she looked enough like Sunny to be her twin sister. But looks can deceive, and I didn't get close enough to put my hands on her." He scratched a match with his thumbnail, cupped it in his hand and bent over the flame. He wasn't wearing a cap and the wind ruffled his cottony hair, standing it up in little spikes. "If I'd of done that," he added, "I'd know for sure."

Lou French half turned, one elbow on the fence. He had on a tweed jacket, buff breeches, cordovan boots, a narrow-brimmed hat with a feather. It would be so nice, Ellen told herself, when Chance could dress like that again. And she'd have a real silk dress. "Exactly what," Lou French asked Chance, "would putting your hands on that horse have proved?"

So smooth. So cool. Even now she couldn't be *sure* she had seen the twitch of the eyelid, the momentary whitening of his knuckles on the fence. Sometimes it was hard to tell twenty-twenty hindsight from wishful thinking.

Chance waited until his cigar was burning well. Then he reminded Lou French that he had ridden Sun River at Gulfstream and Hialeah when she was a three-year-old; won all those races on her. "I got that mare memorized, believe me," he told Lou French. "She was my first big winner too, don't forget. I use to go by her stall at three in the morning, sometimes, just to look in on her and make sure it wasn't all a dream." His Adam's apple jumped as he swallowed, and he jammed his fists into the pockets of his red windbreaker. "Wouldn't surprise me a bit if I could reckonize her blindfolded." He picked at a splinter on the paddock fence and all of them looked out beyond the yearlings at the broodmares on their sunny hill. There were eight or ten mares. Three of them were chestnut-colored, their winter coats shaggy and dull. One of the three had a white stripe down its face, but the other two looked, to Ellen at least, and at least from that distance, exactly alike.

Lou French grinned. "Blindfolded, huh?"

"Sure," Chance said. "What's so funny?"

"Too bad those mares are way out there in that muddy field," Lou French said, still grinning. "Otherwise," nudging Chance with his elbow, "I just might make you give us a demonstration."

"He don't think I can do it," Chance told Ellen in a loud whisper. He waggled his eyebrows, relaxed now—loose, his own real self again—pretending he thought Lou French couldn't hear him. "What the man don't remember about me from all those years ago is I got the touch," and he held up his hands and wriggled his fingers like a circus magician preparing to pluck a hanky from your ear. "What the man don't understand is if you got the touch, you can reckonize anything from out of your past. Paths through the woods, Model A Fords, your first varmint gun, your first good horse or your first good lady." He rumpled her hair so she'd know he didn't mean that part, that it was just a joke. "And you can do it blindfolded and with a sack over your head too, in the middle of the darkest night." He seemed all set to go splashing out through the puddles to the broodmare pasture, but Lou French said that wasn't necessary.

"Of course," Lou French said—joking too? Ellen couldn't tell—"of course I don't believe you can do it, Chance. But I'm going to give you the opportunity to make a fool of yourself if that's what you want to do." Sun River wasn't the only horse he owned that Chance ought to remember, he said. He had another one in the barn. "But ten bucks says you're talking through your hat."

He drew a yellow silk handkerchief from his jacket pocket and held it out to Chance. Playfully but not playfully; shaking it a little, twitching it the way you'd twitch a string in front of a cat to get it to pounce. Chance looked at the handkerchief. Then he turned and winked at Ellen again and told her to start deciding how she wanted to spend the ten he was about to liberate off his old buddy here. Lou French tied the handkerchief over Chance's eyes and then motioned to one of the grooms lounging in the doorway of the nearest barn. He whispered something to the man, who disappeared into the barn, returning a moment later with a stocky little gray horse.

Chance ran his hands up and down all four of the animal's legs and traced the bony outlines of its face with his dark-stained fingers, and after no more than a minute's thought he said, "The gray lead pony, Lou. I don't remember his name, but he got that scar on his hock when that Summer Madness colt of yours kicked him on the way to the starting gate at Hialeah."

The groom raised his eyebrows and whistled. Chance pulled the blindfold loose and grinned until he remembered his teeth and covered his mouth with his hand. Lou French smiled too—and was it just imagination now, or did his eyelid flutter again?—and he opened his pigskin wallet. "Pretty impressive," smoothing a ten between his thumb and forefinger. "To tell the truth, Chance, I didn't think you could do it. The word on you from years back is that you'd lost that touch of yours."

Chance pocketed the ten. He licked his lips; he knew Lou French wasn't talking about the kind of touch that told one horse or one path or one lady from another in the dark. He said, "The word's wrong then, Lou. Some things a man don't ever lose."

Wire fences, six-foot drifts; it had taken him a while, but he'd put two and two together. And so had she. Her first clue had been the article in the *Sporting News*. "Olympus Farm Sells Top Broodmare," the headline read, and the story went on to tell how Lou French had sold Sun River, now in foal to a Triple Crown winner, to Mr. and Mrs. Jason Humble, of Clear Springs, New York, for "a sum reportedly in the neighborhood of $1,000,000." Big deal, the girl had thought at the time, but the article nagged at her mind until she read it again and then a third time. Even so, it wasn't until she saw the TV show that its real meaning and significance had sunk in.

That's my future. Pointing to the mares and foals. If Lou French felt that way—and he had certainly seemed sincere— why would he sell his best mare? Even for a million bucks; he didn't need the money. He had money coming out his ears.

It didn't make sense. He just wouldn't do it, unless . . .

She frowned, sitting in the Vincents' kitchen with the magazine—left behind by one of Ray's friends—spread open on the table, and the little boys' laughter coming to her faintly from the backyard where they played. She tried to imagine a situation in which Lou French might agree to such a sale. No good. He wouldn't do it. But that very night when she was watching TV the answer came to her. The show was a mystery movie; a man switched one racehorse for a slower one that looked like it, and everyone got rich making bets. Pretty slick, she had to admit. And what you could do with a racehorse in its prime you could surely do with a broodmare. When the realization struck her she laughed aloud. Lou French was selling ringers; eating his cake and keeping it too. And Chance . . . ? Her laughter faded. Too bad for Chance who could tell horses apart in the dark. Too bad for Chance who had seen Sun River's double at the Double Deuce last winter.

THE TWO MEN play cards all evening in the library, using a slick new deck with Irish setters on the backs instead of bicycles. More candles, a fire in the huge stone fireplace; bearskin rug on the hearth where Ellen lies, half-dreaming in the flickering light. The walls are lined with leatherbound books, there are carpets from India on the gleaming hardwood floors and hunting scenes above the mantel. Over the door, framed by a pair of antique rifles—flintlocks, Lou French says—is the head of a fine six-point buck. To Ellen, it's a room out of a dream, and she keeps sneaking glances at Lou French, telling herself *I actually know the guy who lives here!* But she does wish Chance would put his hand over his glass and not let Lou French pour him any more brandy. For one thing he'll be sick. And for another, he's playing bad poker, losing almost every hand.

Lou French grins. "Okay, if you're sure," as Chance raises him and raises him again, and he gives Chance a look that

CHANCE

Ellen can't read at all. "You must think I've gone soft," he says, and spreads four jacks and a queen on the table. "Here I sit, sipping whiskey like a Virginia gentleman, fooling most of the people most of the time. But you, Chance, you ought to know better. Scratch the surface and I'm still what I always was, a Nevada cowboy, just like you." He leans back in his leather chair with his snifter of brandy and his blue silk scarf and his tweed jacket the color of young spruce, and he puts his feet up on a little needlepoint-covered stool. "Tell you what." Another grin, this one quick and sharp, a razor slicing flesh from bone. "Here's a chance for you to win back everything I've taken from you tonight." The two of them lock eyes and Ellen knows they are on the edge of something deep-rooted and bitter that she doesn't understand and is helpless to prevent. "You game?"

Chance half rises from his chair. His ruddy face is pale; forehead, nose, chin, one cheek shine in the firelight as if they've been oiled. "Double or nothing."

Lou French smiles pleasantly. It does nothing to ease the tension between them. He riffles the deck; Chance's Adam's apple jumps. "Okay then," Lou French agrees, "double or nothing. Tell me where the word 'buckaroo' comes from and what it means."

Chance's jaw just drops. Still half-standing, hands on the arms of his chair, his sweaty face suddenly pink again as his color returns with a rush. "That's it?" His voice squeaks with relief. And really, Ellen thinks, what kind of a silly bet *is* this? Chance settles back into his chair. "That's really it? That's all I have to do to win?"

Lou French swirls the brandy in his glass. "That's it."

Chance swallows some brandy and gives Ellen a look. "Lou, I'm gonna clean you out!"

Lou French stretches his legs, feet toward the hearth. He's

waiting, he says, and Chance says, "Well, as anybody knows . . ." and then he hesitates, frowning doubtfully. "This has got to be a trick."

Lou French smiles.

It's a trick. Six feet away, Ellen feels the wariness roll off Chance in waves. But he can't back out. He wipes his palms on the thighs of his jeans. "Okay, Lou, I'll bite. 'Buckaroo' comes from *vaquero*, which is Mexican—Spanish, I guess." He glares at Lou French defiantly.

Lou French nods. His wallet has appeared in his hand. "That's half of it, Chance. Now tell me what it means."

Still wary, but beginning to believe again, he watches as Lou French counts out bills from his wallet and adds them to the pile on the table. "Well, shit. It means cowboy, everybody knows that." He waits, one eye on the money and the other on Lou French's face—or so it seems to Ellen—and the tip of his tongue appears, just the very tip end, and he licks his lips like a cat tasting cream.

Lou French just laughs and shoves the money across. "Son of a gun. That's twice today. I guess you *haven't* lost your touch." He is silent until Chance has pocketed the cash—it's about a hundred dollars—and then he says, "Just one thing. I haven't lost mine either. Soft living doesn't make for a soft man, necessarily. It's like apples. The bad rot starts on the inside." The two of them lock eyes and the bitter feeling leaps like a spark between them and then vanishes. Lou French reaches for the brandy bottle. Here's to a bright future; he hopes things will work out. "I do, Chance, I surely do, and I ought to be able to let you know in a couple of weeks at the latest. You and me," he goes on, "we've had our ups and downs, but I think we understand each other now." He holds out his hand. "Just a couple of high-country cowpokes gone wrong, that's all. Both of us ought to be up in the hills right about now, with a couple good rifles and a couple good dogs and a bottle of Wild Turkey, instead of sitting around on our cans down here. Now ain't that right?"

Ellen can't imagine what he means by that. He just isn't the type to say ain't. Chance moves as if to pour himself more brandy, thinks better of it—is his stomach paining him?—and glances at her. "Guess I'll turn in. Sugar, you coming?" He strides from the room without a backward glance, leaving her to follow if she will.

"Chance?"

No answer. A bed with a real canopy, but he turns his back to her.

"Would you tell me what that was all about?"

"Drop it, sugar." He's wearing red-and-gray-striped pajamas, bought new for the trip. So stiff they crackle.

"Chance?"

"Just drop it, I said!" And then, "That bastard. Who needs him?" and he reaches out a skinny arm and snaps off the light. No kiss, no squeeze, no nothing, as if he knows that she'll dream of Lou French, that rich and powerful man. A winter afternoon. Cool golden light strikes the cut-glass punchbowl and breaks into a thousand sparks and needles. Fifty guests at least, down from Washington or up from Atlanta. Important people; they mill around with their champagne and their caviar on little crackers and there's crystal and sterling shining everywhere. She stands there in a real silk dress (the label says); some governor or astronaut chats with her like he's glad she's there, just like he's known her all her life. She talks to him too, laughing at his jokes, liking the feel of the silk against her skin, and she thinks, yeah, I can learn to do this.

And later in the dream she sees the silk dress in a heap on the floor beside a pair of shoes. Real lace curtains at the windows, but they're lined with heavy cloth. Not much light comes through. Just enough. Just enough that in her dream she sees his face, that powerful rich man. She raises herself on one elbow. Her hair brushes his chest and she touches his nipple with the tip of her tongue. Let go, open your hands, the river will take you. And Ellen thinks in her dream, yeah, I can do this part too.

But in the morning Chance is okay. He's fine; he and Lou French have been up for hours when she finally comes downstairs, ashamed to look at either of them, afraid the dream will show on her somehow. They've had breakfast, they've even been on a horseback ride, they swap jokes like the good friends they've been for so long. And on the way home Chance sings along with the radio and holds her hand. Tells her the familiar stories: "That's how it was, sugar. And that's how it's gonna be again, now that me and him are getting back together."

VAQUERO, BUCKAROO. It had been a warning of some kind; another of Lou French's games. And Chance had tried to play. They both had. She hated remembering the way his eyes had followed Lou French's hand as Lou French had taken the money from his wallet bill by bill and laid it on the table; hated to remember the pink tip of his tongue, that quick little wipe across his upper lip; hated to think that her own eyes had very probably followed the money too, that she might very possibly have licked her own lips. Distracted—bought! the both of them!—by a hundred bucks, give or take a few. Deaf and blind to what was really going on.

Fortunately, he'd come to his senses. She knew he had. She pictured the two men face to face in the morning sunshine at the edge of the broodmare field. Both of them angry and both of them scared, although Lou French doesn't show it. And Chance tells him, you know I ain't no angel, never was. But there's limits, Lou. You got to draw the line somewhere.

CHANCE

Lou French goes for his wallet, of course. How much does he offer? A thousand? Two? Chance waves it away. Five, then, my last offer, says Lou, and Chance says it ain't the money. "Matter of fact," reaching into his shirt pocket, "here's what I took off you last night," counting out a hundred or so, "and yesterday afternoon," laying down the last ten. The Rolls is parked there by the fence, or maybe the huge red van. Chance uses the hood for a table and the money flutters there, dull green against the brilliant red, and the breeze plucks at it, lifting the ten, a five, another ten, scattering the bills like leaves at the men's feet. "I don't want your money, Lou, and you know what you can do with your job." And that's when Lou French laughs and cuffs him on the arm. "Hey, Chance, take it easy, you got it all wrong." It's just a little test he's running, on account of what happened down in Florida. No hard feelings, he hopes. "Because you passed with flying colors and I know what happened before wasn't really your fault at all. They set you up and I shouldn't have set you down." But bygones are bygones, aren't they, Chance, and it's okay now, you're my boy again, you've really always been my boy.

Chance wants to believe him. Chance does believe him, singing along with Emmylou Harris on the radio on the drive north. Cold as it is, he has the window down, banging on the pickup's door with his fist. "Old times," he says. "Stick with me, sugar. I'm a lucky buckaroo!"

Buckaroo. A warning: I know you and you know me. Stay bought or die.

Ray Vincent said of course he'd been serious about helping her find work. What did she have in mind? She asked if he knew anyone out west, maybe California? Didn't his sister live there? "I think," with a little smile, "I'd sort of like a change of scene."

Ray nodded. His brother-in-law ran a trucking firm. Maybe

they could use somebody; he'd put in a good word. And within a week it was set. Turlock, California. Bookkeeper for the P&D Freightlines. And sure, she could start in mid-November, if that was what she wanted.

The girl had no idea on earth where Turlock was. All she knew was that California was a long way west of Scott's Run and so was Nevada, so she'd be heading in the right direction. And anyway, Turlock, California, wasn't the place. Phoenix, Arizona, was the place. Get off the bus, grab the gambler's special to Las Vegas and then hitch if she had to, north and west to Cresta. When Lou French came down off the mountain she'd be waiting.

She watched the Double Deuce for a long time, crouched behind some bushes that grew beside the road, but saw no movement except for the animals grazing in the field. No smoke rose from the stone chimney. There was no reason to believe that the cars and pickups parked by the barn belonged to anyone but Lou French and his guests, all of them up there in the high country safely out of the way. Someone could come at any moment, of course; no doubt someone would be along eventually, to feed the stock. But for the moment, she thought, standing cautiously, checking up and down the road for approaching cars . . . for the moment she was safe.

The main barn was large, built of whitewashed logs, with a steep tin roof. It looked deserted. The girl made her way quietly around the outside, trying to see in through a window, but the only one low enough for her to reach offered nothing but a cobweb-blurred glimpse of a rusty pitchfork hanging from a bracket on the wall. However, the door rolled open easily on well-oiled tracks. The girl's mouth was dry. She could feel her pulse racing, but she wasn't afraid. Alert, wary, she took in all the details of everything around her, everything separately and everything at once: littered aisleway, wheelbarrow, hay bales, the rough splintery boards of the walls; smells of dust, horses, leather; soft clucking of a hen somewhere out of sight. But definitely, she wasn't afraid. Happy was more like it—a calm, cool joy that filled her as she stepped inside.

The stalls were all empty, as she had known they would be. Saddle stock and pack animals, all up on the mountain, chickens in the dusty rafters overhead, pigs in the corral, steers in the field, everything where it belonged. Of course there weren't any horses here. She hadn't been foolish enough to expect to find a racehorse or a broodmare—or their twins—carefully hidden away. She climbed the steel-runged ladder to the loft. It didn't take long to find the perfect spot—a space between two hay bales with a view through a knothole of the back door of the house. She could wait there when the time came.

The front and back doors of the house were both locked but she found a window that wasn't and clambered awkwardly over the sill into the large, clean, old-fashioned kitchen. A wood-burning stove! Cold to the touch, though, a reassuring sign. Nothing in the funny little old fridge but five cans of beer and a jar of yellow mustard. French's, of course! Half-closing her eyes, she loaded the counters and the scarred Formica table with bags of chips and pretzels—no, with jars of caviar and olives, the tiny white pickled onions she'd seen advertised in magazines; plates stacked with little sandwiches cut in triangles, arranged in pretty patterns on a pretty tray. She stared through her lashes at the merry glowing stove as someone in a white chef's hat bent to slide a flat pan into the oven. Biscuits. To go with the platter of sliced Virginia ham. As she watched, a cocktail waitress pushed through the swinging door with empty glasses on a tray. A babble of voices and laughter followed her, and the twang of a guitar being tuned. The singer had arrived! You could feel the excitement, even in the kitchen.

"Almost showtime!" says the chef. The waitress grabs her clean glasses and runs, so as not to miss a trick, and the little Mexican maid who's been washing dishes wipes her soapy hands on her apron and presses an ear to the door.

Beyond the door was the living room, of course, and it was just as he had described it to her a hundred times or more: massive stone fireplace at one end, beamed ceiling and dark leather chairs. They'd have to bring in tables from somewhere, though. Heavy oak-plank tables; they'd be covered with white cloths. One table for food, another for booze—bottles and bottles of whiskey and wine, and rows of gleaming glasses. The bartender, a red-haired black man, ladles up champagne punch from a crystal bowl.

Calm and happy, whistling softly between her teeth, the girl walked quietly across the bare pine floor. She paused midway, taking the gun from her purse and turning once full circle, imagining how the room would be. Maybe a stage in that corner? Tables there and there, beneath the row of mounted deer head trophies. The bar with its bottles and punchbowl and long-stemmed glasses . . . ? Beside the fireplace, maybe. And the people—waitresses, bartender, a couple of guitarists in fancy shirts; Lou French's guests in little laughing groups, telling tall stories, they've had a real good time. Their hunt was a success. The smell of roasting venison wafts in from the kitchen every time someone opens the door.

Easy to picture it; easy to picture Chance here, drink in his hand, ruddy face glowing in the firelight as he joins right in. He's part of this, he belongs, he's been a part of it before. He and Lou French, up on this same mountain—another of his stories that she knows by heart. But this one is not one of her favorites. Chance and Lou French and some other guys; pack mules, saddle horses, beautiful guns. Browning Magnums and Mausers, "and a bunch of other imported stuff nobody but a college professor could pronounce," he'd say, "and Jaeger

scopes," but not for him. He never used a scope. Took all the
fun away, put the deer right in your lap, sugar, you might as
well shoot fish in a barrel. And Lou French felt the same.

Up on this same mountain, then, that other time. She'd like
to turn away, but he holds her as he holds the others—his
energy, his open, friendly grin. He refills his glass, his cheeks
glowing red in the firelight as the guests gather round to listen
to his yarn. "Worst luck I ever had," he says, "and not just
me. We're all of us coming up empty. A week goes by, weather's
bad, we're almost out of booze." Then finally, "I get my buck
and the heart surgeon gets his, and one of the other guys, but
poor old Lou, he's skunked. He don't say nothing," Chance
tells his listeners, "but I know he's mad. So just before we're
ready to leave I take him up on Talking Dog Ridge, just the
two of us for one last try, and it's colder'n witchpussy and a
real mean wind. I'm thinking no deer in their right mind's
gonna be out there, when all of a sudden old Lou points his
rifle at the sky and I look up and there's some kind of a great
big bird up there, so high it's just a speck.

"Lou says he ain't going home empty-handed," Chance goes
on. He's in rare form, he loves an audience and the other
guests are hanging on his words. "He asks me what'll I give
if he makes the shot. 'Fifty bucks,' I go, and I figure I'm safe.
I'm a better shot than Lou, but even I couldn't hit that bird
without a scope. But he pulls the trigger, *pow!* And damned
if this great big eagle don't fall right at his feet like he whistled
for it. He had it stuffed, with the fifty-dollar bill I gave him
in its beak. Had it in the lodge, after he got the lodge built,
but some yahoo stole it."

Lou French stands off by himself meanwhile. Not in a
group, not him. An island of quiet in the noisy smoky room,
he stands alone beside the fireplace and the brassy light gathers
around him and singles him out the way the sun gathered in
around Chance in that dusty field in Murphy, Oklahoma, a

lifetime ago, it seems. And then, while she watches, the firelight gathers in on him even more tightly until he glows and flickers like a flame, fading and flaring and changing before her eyes until it seems that what she's seeing is not a crowded room in a ranch house but the desert landscape of that shoot-out picture in the Aberdeen, and the dead cowboy is no longer a stranger. She's seen that high-bridged nose before; the angular cheeks, more salt than pepper in his hair.

Frontier justice, yes indeed. And as the firelight dims and the noise and laughter fade and the warm smells of cooking are replaced by the chill mustiness of an empty house, it seems to her that the other figure in that painting looks familiar too. Raising the barrel of her pistol. A heavy gun, a man's weapon. Using both her hands, she raises the gun to her lips. She closes her eyes and breathes in deeply. The smoke smells sharp and bitter and clean.

6

MRS. LOMAX was right. The Golden Starlite did look like a dive: one of the dumpy little Main Street bars the girl had seen from the bus window when she arrived last night. Palsied neon signs: DRINKS! ENTERTAINMENT! A hand-lettered poster announced that this evening's feature would be The Famous Miss Rita Worthington and Her Country Swing Band. First set at nine thirty, and meanwhile the jukebox was squalling. The girl could hear laughter and the thump and jingle of slot machines even before she opened the door.

Inside, the warm air was thick with the smell of damp sheepskin jackets, smoke, sweat and beer. Men in Levi's and work shirts slouched at the bar. Cowboys, a few hunters, who could tell? They rolled dice for their beers, shaking the leather cup, white cubes skittering on the lacquered wood. Down near the cash register an old Indian woman stared into her empty glass. The only other women in the place were a shovel-faced pair at the back of the room, each of them playing three bandits at once. The ice had melted in their drinks; their cigarettes burned unnoticed to the filters and dropped from the ashtray to the floor. They weren't talking much, but once, as the girl watched, the taller of the two held up a five-dollar bill and called to the bartender—a man in his sixties, too old for Bucky Rowe—for another roll of dimes.

The girl ordered a Seven-Up and asked if Bucky would be in. The man nodded. Ten o'clock or thereabouts. The girl sipped her drink and did her best to avoid her reflection in the cloudy mirror behind the bar. Hair in a stubby yellow ponytail, no makeup, gray sweatshirt, jeans; nobody you'd look at twice—or once if you could help it, she thought, and watched as that face, framed by bottles and reflected bottles, twisted its mouth and scowled at her. Nobody you'd look at twice, but nobody you'd be likely to connect in any way with Lou French either. That much was a comfort. From time to time one of the men would glance her way, but without any real interest, grinning a little to let her know there was action to be had if she was hard up enough to make the first move. After a while she left the bar and carried her glass over to the corner of the low stage near the slot machines.

The speakers and mikes were already in place in front of a metallic-blue drum set. A bull fiddle, still in its canvas case, lay behind the drummer's stool, and a pedal steel stood off to one side of the drums. The girl was pleased that there would be a live band. She sat on the edge of the stage sucking ice cubes and waiting. Minutes crawled by. Nobody noticed her. She leaned back on one elbow, studying the instruments, trying to imagine herself as the girl who would stand up in front of them and sing. No way! Cocktail waitress was bad enough. Either way, they'd think you were a whore.

At twenty past nine the band arrived: five men in white shirts and black pants and vests and red string ties. Two of them carried electric guitars. They plugged in, tuned their instruments, tested the mikes, but the jukebox was still booming and no one at the bar paid any attention to what was going on onstage. But at exactly nine thirty the bartender pulled the plug on the jukebox and the room fell quiet. The drummer began a roll on his snare. The room went dark except for a milky spotlight focused on a small door beside the stage. "Well, folks," the lead guitarist said, "here she is. The moment you've been waiting for!"

Miss Rita Worthington's jet black hair was long and carefully rumpled. She wore a white vest, a black shirt open at the neck to show a bright red scarf, and black pants like the men's, tucked into red and black cowboy boots. A pearl-handled six-shooter rode high in a white holster on her hip. The audience whistled and stamped as she stepped onstage, smiling and tossing her hair. Her eye shadow was precisely the same shade of blue as the drums.

The girl was pleased. Not only was Miss Rita pretty, but it turned out that she had a good strong lonesome voice too—the kind of voice that would sound just right coming out of your radio late at night, with moonlight patterns on the wall or maybe big soft snowflakes against the Airstream's window, the lighted dial of the clock-radio above the bed glowing amber and the music down low:

> *How many arms have held you*
> *And hated to let you go?*
> *How many, how many, I wonder*
> *But I really don't want to know*

And Chance would have had a few, of course, but not too many: "Sugar, leave it and come on to bed. Never saw such a lady for putting things away." But when she'd wake at night she'd *know*. Two paces to the bathroom door, five to the kitchen, light switch on her left at shoulder height. The Airstream itself was twenty paces from the Quonset hut. A trailer—a mobile home, it was called, but it wasn't going anywhere. It still had wheels, but there were no tires on them; the hitch was rusted shut, the hydraulic hoses rotten and crumbling. And there was a fenced-in yard. Flowers? he said. Sure, why not? and sat down with her and looked at seed catalogs. Red ones, he suggested, nice and bright, and she had planted petunias in a bank against the fence, geraniums in pots by the Quonset hut's front door.

Inside the Airstream: a double bed and fold-out couch and a kitchen and a little dining nook, and when they first looked at the place it was really a mess. All kinds of junk left by the previous tenants, odds and ends of this and that, pictures of naked girls torn from magazines and taped to the walls, no frames, just the ragged edges and the tape, everything slaunchwise and cattywumpus to everything else, and some of it pretty disgusting. Go to it, he told her, fix it however you want, but he wouldn't let her paint the bathroom door. POINTERS AND SETTERS, it said. He thought that was pretty funny and so did his friends.

She bought curtains first, red and white checked, and a red shag rug that you could wash in the coin machine in Scott's Run, and a red cover for the bed. The couch was brown and had dark hair-oily patches on the back cushions and smelled like wet dogs so she bought another bedspread to cover it with, but that was *too much* red, so even though Chance said he liked it fine she took it back and got a different one, plaid, with a lot of green and blue. She bought a Sears portable TV, a set of Melmac dishes, and silverware that matched, and made him help her pick everything out. Get what you like, he said— that was early the first year; the repair shop was still doing well. They had plenty of money. Just don't go hog wild, he said, but she said no, you help. It seemed important. If you were somebody with a set of matching silverware you'd helped pick out, you weren't going to just pack up and leave in the night, were you?

Then she bought frames for the motorcycle pictures she'd

cut—not torn—from the *Cycle News*. You could get nice woody-looking plastic ones at the Scott's Run Woolco for about four bucks apiece, and they made all the difference. Chance couldn't believe how nice the place looked, and after a while he even changed his mind about the bathroom door. One morning she woke up and smelled something funny and there he was, covering over the POINTERS AND SETTERS sign with fresh white paint. Happy Anniversary: they'd been together exactly one year to the day.

> *Just let it remain your secret*
> *Cause darlin', I love you so*
> *How many, how many, I wonder*
> *But I really don't want to know.*

Moonlight, snowflakes, and Chance would have had a few, of course, but not too many this time. He flushes the john, the bathroom door opens; fan of light on the ceiling, his black silhouette. And she, she'd be. . . .

And she'd better be keeping her mind on business. It was after ten o'clock, and sure enough, a different man was rinsing glasses behind the bar.

Bucky Rowe looked to be a few years older than Chance. Than Chance would have been. He was short and heavy-boned, with an eagle tattoo on the muscle of his arm. "Chance Griffin?" He reached behind him for a towel and began wiping the glasses he'd just rinsed. "Sure, I knew him." He angled a sharp look at the girl. "Why?"

A little ripple of excitement raised goose bumps on her arms, and something inside her fluttered—a silvery feeling, but it didn't last. She set her empty glass on the bar. The room stank of booze and sweat and smoke; her head ached and her eyes felt full of grit. "He was my . . ." she began, and then stopped, clutching the edge of the bar. "He was what you might call a friend of mine."

"Yeah?" Drying glasses; putting a good polish on them. After a moment he gave the girl another look. Turning things over, fitting them together, making up his mind. "That a Seven-Up?" he asked at last. "You want another?"

"I guess."

Bucky refilled the glass and handed it back to her. "Too bad what happened," he said. "The sheriff came around here afterward, you know. I couldn't tell him anything." He shrugged. "We hadn't kept in touch at all, Chance and me. I heard he was in town here for a day or two last winter, after his father passed, but I didn't see him."

The girl said, "He use to talk about you a lot. About when you and him and the others all worked at the fairgrounds and use to go hunting together and all."

The man raised his eyebrows but offered nothing.

"Did you know him before that?" she asked. "Like around town here or anything? Did you go to his same school?"

Bucky shook his head. "I didn't know him at all till he showed up at the track. He must have been . . . what? Thirteen or fourteen." He paused, poured a Scotch for a customer, frowned. "One thing I'll give him. He was a tough little bastard, even then."

The girl studied Bucky's stocky build and said doubtfully, "Were you a jockey too?"

He laughed. "A shit slinger—a groom. My dad had some old bangtail quarter horses . . . matter of fact, Chance rode for us, off and on. Till," sourly, "he got too busy."

"Well," the girl said, "I guess after that Mr. French guy showed up. . . ."

"Lou didn't have nothing to do with it," he told her sharply. "Lou was all right—still is. A real decent guy. *He* kept coming around. Even after he'd sent his string to California, he'd show up every now and again, hang around the barns and shoot the shit with the guys. But Chance . . ." He half turned away from her, shucking the tops from bottles of beer. "No way. Once that dude left here, he was gone."

"Now wait a minute!" the girl began, but someone interrupted. Was it true that Lou French had gotten his start right here in Cresta?

"Sure." Bucky scooped ice into a glass and grinned at the three or four men who leaned toward him, their backs to Miss Rita onstage. "You aren't going to believe this, but old Lou was raised over in Tonopah; his dad was a miner. And when he first showed up at the fairgrounds, oh, eight or ten years ago I guess, all he had to his name was a crowbait called Slim Slam, an old three-horse International van and a German shepherd dog." He paused, the soda siphon in his hand, thumb poised on the trigger. "All three of them lived in the van, like gypsies." Soda whooshed into the glass. Bucky shook his head. "And look at him now. Up by his bootstraps; worth how many million? Only in America, right?"

Right, the other men agreed, you had to admire a guy like that. "He's at his ranch now," a fat man said. "Up at the lodge, with a bunch of guests. It was in yesterday's *Herald*." Someone said he'd seen Lou French's jet at the Reno airport. Only it wasn't his jet anymore, the fat man said. "Smart as he is he got burned pretty good—taken to the cleaners. And some kind of lawsuit too." "Had to hock his granny," another voice said, and the fat man nodded. "Selling off his breeding stock too, I hear. Guess that's what you get when you do business with A-rabs. But it could have been worse. At least he still gets to use the plane."

The girl scarcely listened. They had it wrong. Bucky had it wrong. Red van with silver letters. General Frank in his glittering brass, Lou French taking the cigar from his lips just long enough to point: *You!*

"Wait a minute," she said again, but Miss Rita's first set had ended and the crowd at the bar had grown noisy. Talk turned from Lou French to guns and dogs. As far as the girl could tell, everyone and his brother was going to be up in the high country that weekend, trying for a deer before the weather closed in for good.

The band played a second long set, and it wasn't until that ended that she had a chance to talk to Bucky again. But at 1 a.m. the jukebox came back on. The guitarists packed up their instruments, Miss Rita finished the last of the bourbon-and-gingers she'd been pulling on all evening, and they left. Most of the crowd left too, then. The girl ordered another Seven-Up.

Bucky Rowe was wiping down the bar. "You still here?"

"About Chance," she said.

"What about him?" Emptying ashtrays in a hurry; he wanted to go home. And so did she. Her headache was worse; the smoke in the room irritated her throat. She coughed. "They shot him. It's just so unbelievable." Her voice wavered and a nerve danced in her cheek. "But it's not like you said. About Lou French and all." She hesitated, staring past Bucky at that yellow-haired stranger's face in the glass. "Is it?"

"Is it what?" he asked impatiently, wiping ashtrays with the same towel he'd used on the bar. "It's just like I said. Lou shows up one day with his old rickety van and his crowbait and his German shepherd, and he's so strapped for cash that he can't afford a stall, much less a decent jock to ride for him. But just look at him now."

The girl shook her head. "He chose Chance. Chance was the rider he wanted."

Bucky looked at her. "He tell you that?"

She nodded.

"Figures. Well, okay. I guess you could say Lou chose him—after John Grill turned him down and Chico Cardozo busted a leg. After that, who'd really care? Lou just grabbed who was handy, and that was Chance."

"I don't believe you." The room was stuffy. She could barely breathe. "He'd just hired out to work for Mr. French again." She grabbed Bucky's wrist. "Just that very day he got killed. We were going to Virginia; he was going to be a partner in the deal. And then pow! I mean, it just seems so weird."

The bartender looked down at her hand—wiry fingers, chipped dark-red nail polish—and his own with its coarse black hairs on the back. "Just what the hell are you suggesting?"

"Nothing!" She jerked her hand away. "I don't know! I just feel like . . . Are you sure there isn't anything? Any little unimportant thing you didn't tell the cops?"

"Sorry." He looked at her, right at her, with no friendliness at all. "I hadn't seen Chance in years. And that was okay by me. Do I make myself clear? If Lou really did take him on again—and all I have's your say-so about that—well," carefully folding the towel and laying it neatly over a rack, "all that proves is that even a smart man can make a dumb move every now and then."

The girl licked her lips. "But you two were friends! He use to tell me. . . ."

"No." He looked at her and shook his head. "I'm sorry, miss, I really am, but Chance Griffin was no friend of mine. If you want to talk to somebody about him, maybe you ought to see his wife."

The girl stared down at the lacquered wood of the bar, studying the dark pattern of the grain. "Wife?"

"Ex-wife, I guess. Or maybe not, I really don't know." Bucky yawned and rubbed his eyes. "You mean he didn't tell you?" When she didn't answer he shrugged. "Figures. Well, not too many people do know about it, I guess, because she keeps it quiet, but Chance used to be married to Rita. You know, the singer who was here tonight."

Carefully: "Wife?"

Bucky shrugged. "Or ex-wife." Rita was a local girl, he

went on. "A lot older than Chance. Hell, she's a lot older than me. It was just one of those things, I guess; they got hitched down in Florida, but it didn't last. I never heard whether they ever really got divorced or not, but Rita's been back here working the local clubs for the past four–five years now. She goes up to Lou's; that party he throws every year when the season ends. Her and the band put on a little show."

The Indian woman by the cash register pointed wordlessly at her glass. Bucky opened a fresh bottle of orange juice, reached behind him without looking and came up with the gin. The silver measuring spout winked like a star when he poured.

Old girlfriends, even hookers—you had to expect things like that. But a wife! How could he not tell her? How could she not know?—when she'd known him so well for so long! Wouldn't you think it would have *showed* on him in some way? The girl took a deep breath, held it for a long moment and then said evenly that she guessed she'd try to talk with Rita.

Bucky slid the woman's drink across the bar and nodded. "She lives in Boreen. It's not too far."

The jukebox had fallen quiet, but the girl's head continued to pound. "Boreen." She cleared her throat. "Yeah, maybe I'll do that."

Bucky drew a glass of beer from the tap and drained half of it in one long swallow. "Don't know how much help she'll be. Like I said, they went their separate ways. And Rita, well . . ." He shrugged. Rita could be touchy. But it couldn't hurt to try. And then he called out to the slots players that it was almost closing time. They'd better let him build them a last one for the road.

7

SHE WOKE the next morning with a raw throat and a shallow, hacking cough. Feverish, disoriented—*wife?* A cold gray rain still fell. As she left the Aberdeen she looked west toward the mountains, but they were lost in cloud.

The Crossroads was full of men in red jackets or orange vests: faint-hearted hunters waiting for the sun to shine. She recognized the fat man from the Golden Starlite, forking up pancakes and syrup and describing his new rifle to his companions. A Champlin thirty-thirty, she heard him say, with a hand-checkered walnut stock. It had set him back eight hundred bucks. He glanced up briefly as she passed his table, and then went back to his breakfast.

Mrs. Lomax poured coffee and set the carton of half-and-half on the counter. "Any luck?"

"Some." The girl hunched over her cup, avoiding the woman's eyes. It was stupid to have come here again this morning.

Get up on your feet, she told herself. Act like you got some sense; get out while you can. Because it wasn't going to work. None of it. It just wasn't possible, crazy as she'd been acting, that nobody had noticed. She'd left a trail like a four-lane highway, and *anybody* could have been there in the Starlite last night, back in some smoky corner. She knew all about rich guys like Lou French, had read about them and seen them on TV. They had people everywhere . . . people with no other job in this world but to keep their eyes and ears open for the boss. She frowned, trying to think who it might have been. Some cowboy-looking character. Dropping quarters into the jukebox with his back to the bar while she did everything but come flat out and accuse Lou French of murder.

Her skin crawled. She looked up and saw that Mrs. Lomax was smiling at her. "You want your eggs over easy again this morning?"

Was she . . . ? Could she be the one? What little appetite the girl had brought with her had vanished. "A tad more coffee, that's all." Her voice sounded tight and she was sweating—not just nervous, as she'd been in the bus depot, but scared. Truly scared, for the first time since she'd made up her mind to do what had to be done. She didn't give a hoot in hell about Mr. and Mrs. Jason Humble, rich folks from Clear Springs, New York. If they weren't smart enough to check up on what their money was buying, that was their problem. And if Lou French was smart enough to take them to the cleaners, more power to him. Because Chance was dead and he was going to stay dead and all of a sudden she wanted to stay alive. It felt to her as if she was losing her grip on something she hadn't even known was there. "I'm just not very hungry," she said.

Mrs. Lomax leaned across the counter and touched her forehead. "You feel okay, hon? You better try and eat a little something, some toast at least. Or at least drink a glass of juice."

The girl drew back. *Was she . . . ?* Of course she wasn't, but still. Last night's headache had returned. The girl couldn't think. Married, and never a word in all those years. And here she was, acting like a fool and probably fooling nobody. Go on, get out. Put it all behind you and just go.

Mrs. Lomax was waiting. "Juice," the girl said, figuring it would slide down as easily as coffee. "And while you're at it, I sure could use a couple aspirins."

The woman nodded. "I thought you looked feverish. There's a real mean flu going around."

Flu? The girl coughed. It hurt all the way to her fingertips, but her head cleared for a moment. Bucky had been wrong about Lou, about his arrival at the fairgrounds and the way he'd chosen Chance. Wrong or a liar, one or the other. So why should she take his word as gospel on Chance's relationship with Rita? Bucky was obviously a man with an ax to grind, she told herself. Probably he was jealous of Chance's success, as so many others had been. She swallowed her juice and aspirin and shoved aside the thought that perhaps she really was coming down with something more than just a cold. She could see Miss Rita this afternoon, get the story straightened out and be on a westbound bus by suppertime. Ditch the gun somewhere. No one would know. It was scary to think how close she'd come.

She stayed in her room for the rest of the morning, waiting for her head to stop pounding and her throat to ease and for the rain to quit. But by noon she felt no better and the only change in the weather was that the temperature had dropped so that the rain was mixed with sleet. A wife. Well, she would see. And afterward . . . well, she would see about that too. But she took the forty-four from its hiding place and looked at it, and at the six cartridges in their little plastic bag. What you want with that cannon, girl? the one-eyed man had asked. And laughed when she said, To kill a guy.

The muzzle of the gun felt cold against her front teeth. It had a cheap sour taste, like the birthstone ring she'd taken from the Woolco in Galveston when she was ten. She'd carried the ring out of the store in her mouth, and little gold flakes had stuck to her tongue.

Ten past. Twelve thirty. She took two more aspirin, reached for the tight orange jeans. Flimsy boots, yellow blouse, she fluffed her yellow hair. She had no idea why. Her other clothes were warmer and more comfortable but it felt right to her to visit Miss Rita dressed this way. Shrugging into the white vinyl jacket, she hung out the DO NOT DISTURB and left the hotel quietly by the service door.

There was more sleet than rain by the time she reached the highway. No traffic; it was two o'clock or later before she arrived, light-headed and woozy, in Boreen. A man at the Quik-Stop in the center of town knew where Rita Worthington lived and told her the way.

The house was lemon yellow. A gravel path looped between withered flower beds and patches of lawn where the grass stuck up in stiff gray-brown clumps through the ice. At eye level on the door was a silver knocker shaped like a guitar. The girl plucked at it with cold stiff fingers, gave up after a moment and thumped on the door with her fist. There was no answer, but a pink Mustang with the license plate RITA stood in the carport. The girl knocked again and this time thought she could hear somebody moving around. "Miss Worthington!" she called hoarsely. "Miss Worthington? Are you there?"

No answer. The wind whipped the sleet and rain in spiral gusts, but the girl was sweating heavily inside her vinyl jacket. Just nerves, she told herself. Not fear; she was past fear now. And not flu either. "Miss Worthington!" When the door swung open she staggered forward and would have fallen if the woman hadn't caught her by the shoulders.

"All right, all right!" Miss Rita's hair was in rollers, her eyelids puffed and red. Without makeup her cheeks were deeply seamed. "Whatever you're selling," she told the girl, giving her a little push back toward the door, "I'm not in the market for it today."

"I'm not selling anything." The girl steadied herself and squared her shoulders. "I just want to talk to you."

"I'm not dressed," Miss Rita snapped. But then an odd look passed over her face. "Oh Lord! I'll bet you're here about the fan club."

The girl's legs wobbled; there were noises in her ears. *Find out . . . be it.* Water dripped from her jacket, pat-pat-pat on the clean yellow tile floor of Miss Rita's entry hall. It was hard, all of a sudden, to keep her eyes focused, and she didn't want anything in the world quite as much as she wanted to sit down. "Sure," she said. "The fan club." And she smiled.

"Oh Lord!" Miss Rita grabbed at the sides of her head where the biggest rollers were. "Oh kiddo, let's get you out of that wet coat and get you comfortable." Then, with a quick, nervous little glance, "Weren't you supposed to come last week? I was looking for you then. It's on my calendar."

The girl shook her head. The room steadied, her vision cleared. "No," she said. "This was the day they told me to come." Adding after a moment, "It's on my calendar."

Miss Rita frowned, patted her hair, shrugged. Oh well. The important thing was that someone had shown up. She hung the vinyl jacket in the coat closet and led the way into the living room, apologizing for having confused the dates, for not being dressed and ready, for the house looking like a cyclone had hit it. She sat the girl down on a plump gold sofa. "Excuse me. Make yourself at home. I'll only be a minute."

The girl sat stiffly on the edge of the couch. Yellow flowers on the chairs and curtains; a huge Zenith color TV. The rug was deep and soft. So many framed pictures so close together on the walls it was as if they'd been laid on with a trowel, and the shelves beside the fireplace were crammed with vases and figurines. *Her* house, she thought. *Her* living room. *His* wife. It might very well be true. But now that the shock was over she didn't feel much of anything one way or another.

The past was the past after all. In fact, her mind drifted unaccountably from Chance and Miss Rita to Ginger Holmes, digging ditches back in West Virginia because some yahoo had pushed him just a little too far.

She remembered in particular a January night two years ago when Chance had turned up missing—late for supper, then very late for supper. Nine thirty, quarter to ten and no sign of him. Out drinking, she supposed, and he'd found a card game or he was rolling dice, hell-bent to blow the profit he'd made on an engine rebuild he'd finished just the day before.

His life, Ellen tells herself, his business how he runs it, but the evening wears on and she's cleaned everything in the Airstream that needs cleaning and some things that don't, and she's watched a cop show and the eleven o'clock news and still he isn't home. His life, his business, but she's uneasy. For one thing, he'd been drinking most of the afternoon, since long before he announced that he was going out. And for another, he'd taken one of the bikes instead of the pickup and it has begun to snow. She can just picture it: the Suzuki wrapped around a tree trunk somewhere and Chance hanging from a limb twenty feet above the ground. Waiting for her. Knowing she'll come. Sugar, you and me.

Of course she doesn't really think he'll have an accident. He's too good a rider. But there are other people on the road. Crazy yahoos, you never know what they're going to do. When eleven thirty comes and still no word she puts on her heavy coat, coaxes the old pickup to start and sets out to find him, whatever trouble he's into.

The bars in Scott's Run first. No luck. But then at the Redtop Roadhouse on the way to Charles Town she finds someone who's seen him. With a bunch of guys, looked like maybe from the racetrack, one of them a big tall redheaded colored guy. So she drives on through the snow, down the narrow back streets in the colored part of town, and sure enough, there's the Suzuki in the shed beside Ginger's panel truck.

Ginger's wife Delois and four of the kids are watching TV in the living room. Ellen, kneeling to pet the old blue-tick hound that rouses itself to greet her, asks, "Chance here?"

Delois doesn't seem particularly glad to see her. "Was," she says, her heavy dark face impassive. "But he lef'. Ginger in the kitchen, though. You can go on back."

She finds him seated at the table, absorbed in wrapping the shank of a tiny fishhook with electric-blue thread. Bright-colored feathers, wire, snips of wool and silk lie spread out before him. He glances up when she comes through the door and gives her a sad-eyed smile that drops her heart right down into her socks. Chance is in real trouble of some kind; she can read it in his face. Straddling a chair she stares at him across the littered table.

"You want a cup of coffee?" Without waiting for an answer he sets the kettle on a burner, gets down a cup from his wife's neat cupboard, opens the can of Maxwell House. Stalling. Jesus God, she thinks. Something terrible has happened. Chance has run off with a Charles Town whore. Either that or dropped dead, one or the other, and she feels herself go cold all over: *what am I going to do?* Knowing that she has no life without him; knowing there's nothing she *can* do, can ever do. Except wait, of course. So she waits in silence while Ginger makes coffee, opens a box of HiHo's and pours himself a beer. He is careful not to meet her eyes. At length he says, "Chance and my boy Willie makin' a run."

Ellen hadn't known that Willie ran shine but it doesn't surprise her any. He's Ginger's oldest, a handsome light-skinned boy of seventeen or so, in trouble off and on since he was ten. He wears flashy clothes, always seems to have a fast car to drive, and for more than a year now he's been cultivating Chance, showing up from time to time at the Quonset hut, sometimes with hubcaps or a battery to sell but more often just to talk. Chance's stories about the sweet life down in Florida—Willie Holmes can listen to them by the hour. Chance says that Willie isn't really bad, just wild, but Ellen's not so sure. And now she realizes suddenly that Ginger isn't so sure either. She can see it in his eyes. "Since when does Willie go partners with anybody?" she asks.

"He don't." Ginger refills her cup and thumbs open another can of beer. "Listen, honey, don't you worry about Chance. He ain't mixed up in this, really. Me and him had a few drinks at the Redtop early this evening, and then he come by here to look at that bumper hitch I welded on John Campion's Scout, and he just stepped in for a sec to say hi to Delois and the kids . . . and speak of the devil," smiling over Ellen's shoulder, "look who's here."

The little boy Bubba isn't quite two—the youngest, except that Delois is pregnant again. So much for lucky number seven. "Scuse me," Ginger says to Ellen, and holds out his arms. Bubba climbs into Ginger's lap and from there onto his shoulders, steadying himself with fistfuls of rust-red hair. Ellen rests her chin on her fists on the back of her chair, and she can almost see the dusty Texas streets, hear the men's laughter and the squeals of the women, smell the garlic and onions. Paco's Bar. Merle Haggard and Johnny Paycheck from behind the beaded curtain in the doorway. Football-shaped plastic beads, red, yellow and green. Sometimes she'd count them while she waited for Mama. She and Jimmy Lee. She'd rock him in his little wagon, try to interest him in the strings of bright beads, in shiny pebbles, passing cars, anything. The movies were better. Sometimes when the cartoons came on he'd laugh, just like an ordinary kid. Even then she'd been thinking of running away. Thinking maybe she'd take Jimmy with her and they'd go to Disneyland.

"My brother used to do me that way," she tells Ginger. "Like I was a jungle gym."

"When he was this age?"

"In a manner of speaking." She looks down, picking at a scrap of red wool on the table in front of her. The kitchen is quiet. Bubba settles drowsily in his father's arms. Snowflakes pile up in broad white U's on the bottoms of the windowpanes above the sink. The faucet drips once—*plonk!*—into a glass half-filled with water and the sudden hum of the refrigerator seems unnaturally loud, filling the warm room and traveling through the floor as a faint vibration that Ellen feels through the soles of her boots. She remembers the welfare lady and the visiting nurse with her blue-bound book full of pictures of unborn babies. Chromosomething damage. The nurse pointing to a page and then the sharp hiss of her mother's indrawn breath. "It ain't—it isn't my fault!"

Ellen says, "I want to know about Chance."

"Yeah." Ginger takes a deep breath, puffs his cheeks and lets the air out slowly through clenched teeth. "Like I said, we had a couple drinks and then he come by here. You know how he is, just stepped in for a minute for a quick one, and then Willie shows up in that new Charger of his, and him and Chance get to talkin' bout this and that and Chance says can he drive the Dodge. And Willie says sure." He shrugs. "And so they taken off. I speck they be back pretty soon." His voice trails away. "Floyd's with them."

"Floyd?" Fifteen years old; Ginger's second son. An honor student, a big kid, just a sophomore but already a starter on all the high school varsity teams. Already being contacted by college football scouts. He talks about studying the law, but lately Ellen has begun to see him in downtown Scott's Run, hanging on corners with a bunch of hoody-looking boys on weekday mornings when he ought to be in school. And now this. Of course, it might mean nothing at all.

"Don't you worry," Ginger tells her. He shifts the sleeping Bubba higher onto his shoulder and reaches for his glass of beer. "They be along." Ellen looks at his broad kind face, his funny orange hair sticking up in clumps where the child grabbed it, and just for a moment she is angry—not just angry but very angry—at Chance. Life isn't a crapshoot, pie doesn't fall from the sky and it isn't fair that decent, careful, Godfearing Ginger should be dealt a hand like this.

She says, "Maybe I could tell Chance to stay away from Willie."

Ginger shakes his head. "Wouldn't do no good, not as far as Willie goes, but thank you. Maybe Floyd . . ." he adds, under his breath as if she isn't really supposed to hear. "Damn. I just don't know." And then, looking down at the sleeping child in his arms: "Lot of things I don't know; lot of things don't nobody know, and maybe we better off," but Ellen isn't listening to him. She's listening to the rumble of the powerful Dodge engine; watching for, yes! there it is! the blue-white sweep of headlights in the snow as the car pulls around behind the shed out of sight of the road. "They're here!" she cries and runs to the door to meet them as they come in, the three of them cold and laughing, yelling for Delois to fix them something hot to eat. And Chance, happy and excited and just drunk enough not to wonder what she's doing there, grabs Ellen and kisses her. "Hey! Guess what, sugar, that poor sucker Willie owes me fifty bucks!" Some bet or other. She never did find out what it was.

Miss Rita was certainly taking her own sweet time about changing her clothes. Steadying herself with one hand on the chintz-covered arm, the girl rose carefully from the couch and studied the photos on the wall beside the fireplace. Looking for Chance, of course, but she didn't find him.

Most of the pictures were of slick-haired men in cowboy

gear. Some of them were holding guitars. Most of them had signed their names but they were nobody she'd ever heard of. Only one picture was of any real interest: five guys in jeans, down jackets and three-day stubbles, holding rifles and standing over the carcass of a deer. There was no way she could be sure, because of the beard, but she thought one of the men just might be Lou French. The girl studied that photo for a long time. And then Miss Rita reappeared, in yellow pants and a yellow and black fuzzy bumblebee shirt, her dark hair carefully rumpled.

She had a stack of pictures with her, glossy blowups of her and the band. "Like 'em?" She gave the girl a smile that, at a distance, could have passed for the one she'd used onstage. Up close it wasn't so good. Up close it looked hungry and it made the girl's flesh creep. Get the hell out, she told herself. All the way out; forget the whole thing. For a minute she thought she really might go.

Miss Rita said, "Come on out to the kitchen, kiddo. I'll rustle up some grub."

The kitchen was small, and a little cramped because of the huge avocado-green GE dishwasher that stood with its back to the sink. There wasn't really room for a built-in, Miss Rita told the girl, "and you know those dinky little portables. Don't work worth a damn. But I don't guess you're here to talk about housekeeping, are you." She set her photos on the round green Formica table and pulled out a chair for the girl, who sank into it gratefully. "Be right with you. I forgot my fountain pen."

The pen was for autographing the pictures. It had a special nib. Miss Rita had bought it when she first found out about the club. "People have always admired my signature," she said. "Now I'll really give them something to look at."

She would autograph the pictures while they were eating, she went on, and then the girl could take the pictures back to her club and the members could buy them at a special rate of two dollars apiece. "If there are any left over your club could sell them for two fifty and make a profit." Opening bread wrappers, packages of baloney, jars of pickles and mustard as she talked: "I thought a dollar fifty at first, but you can say you witnessed me signing them. You can vouch that it was really me, and I did it by hand, not with a stamp the way some people do." She smiled again. "I think it's worth an extra fifty cents or so, don't you? To have it verified that it really is my personal handwriting?"

The girl sat speechless, elbows on the green table and chin in her hands. She had given up even trying to think; her brain lay in her skull like a stone and all she knew was that she'd let things go too far. The woman went on, talking rapidly, punctuating her words with nervous little laughs and tosses of her head, spreading mayonnaise and mustard, fiddling with the lid of the pickle jar. Maybe fifty cents extra was too much? For the club members anyway? Maybe twenty-five cents was more reasonable? She didn't want to rip off her fans, after all; she wasn't like some people. Then, before the girl could respond, she shook her head. "Oh, what the hell. Why charge extra at all? A dollar fifty. How's that?"

"Fine." The girl's voice sounded as if it were coming from miles away. "Just fine," she said, and sneezed.

Miss Rita peered at her. "Are you okay? I surely do appreciate you coming out here on a day like this, but sounds to me like you should've stayed in bed."

The girl nodded and sneezed again. She watched as Miss Rita piled sandwiches on a plate, poured two glasses of orange juice and laced one with a shot of gin. They ate in the living room, the TV going with the sound off, and while she ate, Miss Rita signed pictures and talked about the bands she'd sung with and the places she'd worked. Hotels, nightclubs; she pointed with her pen to each of her souvenirs. A drinking cup from the Ponderosa Ranch. "I did a gig there once." And a commemorative vase—she pronounced it vahz—from Chowchilla, California, that she said Mike Savage had given her. She mentioned this as if the girl should know who Mike Savage was and what Chowchilla was famous for, and the girl nodded helplessly and sneezed and said, "Nice."

"Oh, it's nothing." Miss Rita tossed back her hair. Her smile was better; her color too. She drained her glass and excused herself to make a refill. "O-jay, there's nothing like it," she said when she returned. "Here," handing the girl a framed bronze plaque. "Take a look at this."

The plaque was engraved SOUVENIR OF CRESTA CO. FAIR. "Me and the band do a few numbers every night for the entire two weeks of the festivities. We've been doing it for years," she added, and there was real pride in her voice. "Since way back when they still had the horse racing. I'm what you might call a real tradition around here."

The girl didn't answer right away. She had been looking again at all the ashtrays and salt and pepper sets and china cootchy dancers, and all of a sudden there it was, on a shelf between a black and white porcelain cat and something that might have been a bowling trophy: a little wooden deer that nobody on earth but Chance could have carved. A young buck in velvet; clear white pine, six inches high at the shoulder. Tense, wary, ready to run or fight, he stood poised on delicate little legs no bigger around than pencil leads, with every muscle, every tendon, sharp and clean. And he looked at the girl— right at her, it seemed—as if she were a little wooden figure too.

She looked back at him. She made herself small, a white pine statue, a matchstick, a thorn, a splinter in his heart. Chance. Oh, Chance. The stained blade of his knife. The way he'd turn the wood, the long pale paring curling down.

True, then. No doubt about it anymore.

"I was saying . . ." Miss Rita nudged the girl's arm. "I was *saying*, I'm a real tradition in these parts."

"Oh." Not thinking; staring at the deer. "Oh. Well, you sure don't look that old."

The briefest pause; a sharp intake of breath. "I'm *not!*" Miss Rita snapped. "I started young."

Me too, the girl thought wearily. And what now? She looked down at the photos all signed by hand in special ink by The Famous Miss Rita Worthington who was or had been Mrs. Chance Griffin, and she wished she really was who the woman wanted her to be, and that she really could do what she thought she was going to do. Because she liked Miss Rita. It made no sense, it was the last thing in the world she would have expected, but it was true. She liked Miss Rita, who was a good singer who deserved a fan club if anyone did, and for the life of her she couldn't think of any painless way to turn the conversation around to what she had come to find out.

"I wasn't always on the leaky-roof circuit, you know." Miss Rita had finished her second drink by that time and was well into a third. "I've had gigs in Miami and Tampa, down in Florida, you know, and in New Orleans and Dallas, a lot of big towns. Hotels and supper clubs, very high-class places; I was on my way to Nashville two different times, to cut a record, but circumstances intervened." She rattled the ice in her glass and smiled. "It's been a while, I'll tell you, but it sure looks like the breaks are going to go my way again. Between your club and that talent scout . . . did I mention him to you yet?"

The girl closed her eyes. "No." Things were happening too fast. There was no solid ground, nothing to grab onto when it all caved in beneath her. She swallowed hard, fighting nausea.

It was true, Miss Rita told her. "You go on back to your club and spread the word: Miss Rita's going to Vegas!"

"Great." A thick whisper. The girl cleared her throat. "Great!"

Miss Rita nodded. "This guy, he's been to the Starlite on three separate occasions just in the last month. He's from this club in Vegas; he's been taping my act. He's real impressed with me. All we're waiting on is the final okay from his boss, and when that happens they'll fly me down there in a private plane for a personal audition. He'll be here again tonight and I expect he'll give me the word then about when the audition'll be." Her smile was blinding. "Oh Lord! I'm so overdue for something like this, I just can't wait!"

"I hope it works out." And she did. She let her gaze travel slowly over the photos on the wall, the cut-glass bud vases on the mantel, the soundless rainbow flicker of the TV screen, and then she sighed and asked Miss Rita very politely if it was true that she used to be married to Chance.

Miss Rita just stared with her mouth open a little and her lips pooched, getting ready to shape some word. Vegas, more likely than not. And then all the color just *fell* out of her face. It was, the girl thought dimly, like seeing mercury drop in a thermometer when you set it on an ice cube on a summer day.

"No," Miss Rita said. "I most certainly was never married to anyone of that name."

The girl was ready for her. Without a word she reached up, undid the chain from around her neck, and held out the wooden horse head. It lay on her palm with the burned side next to her skin. Ears pricked, mane curling in an imaginary wind, nostrils flared—you half expected it to whinny.

Miss Rita looked as if she expected it to bite her. "Who in hell *are* you?" Short and sharp. "What the hell are you doing in my house?"

"Chance," the girl said. "He was . . ." and she stopped.

Miss Rita set her empty glass carefully on a coaster on the TV and rubbed her eyes, carefully, because of the mascara. "You have misrepresented yourself," she said, "and I ought to throw you out of here on your fanny. I ought to call the cops. As a matter of fact," taking a step toward the wall phone, "I think I may just do that." But then she stopped and her shoulders seemed to sag a little. She gave the girl a weary smile. "Oh, what the hell. I guess I knew all along you weren't here about the fan club. It *was* last week. They stood me up." She ran the tip of her tongue over her upper lip. "So," she said after a minute. "You were Chauncey's girlfriend."

The girl nodded, pressing the sharp points of the wooden horse's ears into the ball of her thumb. Chauncey. "You could say that."

"And you've come all the way from West Virginia just to talk to me about him."

"You could say that." And you could, she thought. It made as much sense as, To kill a guy.

Miss Rita snorted. "I'd have saved the plane fare," she said tartly, and then, reaching out to touch the girl's arm, "I'm sorry. I shouldn't have said that."

"S'okay." Her throat hurt. Her head felt enormous. "I guess when you get divorced. . . ."

Miss Rita closed her eyes. The skin on her neck was loose and crepey; she was forty-five if she was a day. "He told you about me?"

You and me, sugar. They can have the rest. "Why else would I make the trip?"

"Beats me." Miss Rita shrugged. "Chauncey always was a law unto himself."

"Did you see him last December?"

"Indeed I did. I damn near died of shock, too—him turning up like that after all those years. It was because I helped arrange his father's funeral," she added. "Tom Griffin might have drunk more than was good for him but he was always real decent to me. Not," with a sniff, "like some I could name. But he didn't stay. Wouldn't even take time for a beer, and if you knew Chauncey . . ." She smiled apologetically, hands spread, rings winking on her fingers. "Sorry. I guess you did know him. Otherwise you wouldn't be here, would you."

And the girl said softly, no. Otherwise she wouldn't.

"If it's about his death . . ." Miss Rita paused, watching the girl closely. "If it's about that . . . look, kiddo, I'd like to help, but I just can't tell you much. The cops came here. I mean, just because I was married to him once, like I should know who killed him." She gave a little yip of laughter. "Not that I wasn't tempted myself, on occasion. Not seriously, of course! But he could be a stinker. And then it turned out to be just a couple of punks. Didn't surprise me one bit, that part."

"Why?" the girl asked.

"Why?" Miss Rita frowned, then shook her head. "Just didn't. Never mind. Forget I said that. You want to come on back in the kitchen? I think maybe I could use another glass of juice."

The girl followed her unsteadily. "Those punks didn't kill him," she said from the doorway. Her sore throat seemed to extend from her molars to somewhere deep in her chest. "It was somebody else."

Miss Rita had been about to cap the gin bottle. Instead, she splashed another ounce into her glass.

"Kills the germs," the girl said.

"He tell you that?"

"About twice a week for almost three years."

Miss Rita laughed nervously. "Don't tell me they're going to reopen the investigation." When the girl didn't respond: "Oh no you don't! You're not pulling me into anything like that! I've got my career to think about! I already told the sheriff everything I knew, which wasn't much, believe me. I can't afford to have people get the wrong idea now."

The girl said bitterly, "No way they're reopening the investigation. I wish they would, but it just isn't going to happen.

And nobody's going to get the wrong idea, either. Nobody'll get *any* idea—who's going to know but you and me?"

"Nothing's going to stand in my way this time." Miss Rita tasted her drink, added still more gin and tasted it again. "I'm only thirty-five. I've got plenty of good years left. I can make it!"

"Just talking to me won't change that," the girl said. "Please. We won't even talk about who killed him. We'll just talk about Chance himself, what he was like when you knew him. An hour of your time, that's all I'm asking, and then I'll go away and never bother you again. I promise."

Miss Rita sipped her drink. "I don't know," she said. "I guess something like that couldn't hurt." Her eyes searched the girl's face. "An hour," she said, "and then you'll go?"

And the girl said yes. Then she'd go.

8

THREE MILES west of Boreen the road hooked north and in-
tersected Route 212. Miss Rita turned left and they began to
climb, winding through mist-shrouded pines and aspens toward
Littleboy Pass. The girl sank low in her seat on the passenger's
side of the pink Mustang as they approached the Double Deuce
and didn't even glance to the left again until the gates were
safely behind her. She had made up her mind not to mention
Lou French's name at all, unless Miss Rita brought it up.

They had been driving for almost an hour—through the
towns, out to the fairgrounds, places he'd lived and worked,
missing pieces of the puzzle. Miss Rita had known his whole
family and hadn't thought much of them either, even if old
Tom Griffin *was* a sweet old guy who'd always treated her
decent. "It was the least I could do, helping with his funeral,"
she said. "He was family, in a way; my own folks passed on
years ago. I wanted him buried nice." But he hadn't amounted
to a hill of beans, Tom hadn't. None of them had, until Chance.
"No drive, no ambition. But Chauncey, he was different. Not
better, mind you, but different."

Every so often Miss Rita would pull over and point to something: that was where he and his friends used to play ball,
that was where they'd have picnics sometimes, or bonfires, or

set off fireworks on the Fourth of July. They'd swiped candy
from this store, snuck into that movie theater the back way;
yeah, she guessed that's where he went to school. "It's been
so long. But that's the school, all right. He must've gone there,
and then high school in Iron Springs until he quit."

The girl took it all in silently, waiting.

Nothing.

Nothing was left of the house where he'd lived. An empty
lot near the edge of town. The girl had made her way through
the frozen weeds and the junk and the old boards to the place
where the house had stood. Broken bottles, spent cartridges,
the pop tabs off a million cans of beer. Fire? she asked. Miss
Rita shook her head, shivering and hugging herself in her furry
coat, breathing ghosts on the cold wet air. "Just collapsed,
kiddo. The Griffins were poor."

"But what was he *like?*" the girl asked in a thin voice. Her
head felt loose and light, the bubble in a carpenter's level. Her
knee was killing her. And Chance . . . The places he'd hung
out; where his house had stood. Nothing. He might as well
never have been. She might as well have imagined him. She
said, "I need to know!"

Miss Rita considered. "Things came too easy to him," she
said at last. "He could've been an artist, the way he could
draw and carve, but he didn't want to work at it. And the
same with riding too. He'd rather fool around, him and his
friends; go off hunting or they'd play cards and drink all day,
see who could tell the biggest lies. No contest there," she
added. "He'd win in a walk. And there were times, I swear,
when it seemed like he believed those stories himself—couldn't
tell what happened from what he said had happened."

The girl sneezed. Colored lights exploded in her head. *You!
You're the one I. . . .*

Miss Rita said she'd known him from the time he was a
little short-pants kid. "And he never changed. Always playing

the fool, never stuck with anything, but he did have a way about him, didn't he? His brother Sammy, the one that was lost in the war, he used to weed the garden for my parents. I was living with them then. And Chauncey used to tag along. He loved to hear me sing." She smiled. "Even then. And he used to vow he'd marry me. You know the way kids are."

They drove on past the Double Deuce, past the gates to another ranch, the slick icy road twisting among trees and beside banks. Miss Rita touched the brake and peered intently into the curtain of freezing mist, leaning so far forward that her chin almost touched the steering wheel. "Ah! Here it is."

A turnout, its entrance almost hidden by buckbrush and scrub pines. The Mustang's wheels crunched on loose gravel; a narrow lane opened into a small parking lot. Miss Rita nosed the car up to the guardrail and shut off the engine.

"I guess this is far enough."

They got out, bending their heads against the wind that whipped up out of the canyon below. "Too bad about the weather," Miss Rita said. "When it's clear you can see a good long ways from this ridge. It's a pretty view." She pointed out into the cold fog and the gathering dark, naming invisible peaks: Mount Loren, Mount Hatch, Old Billy's Nose. "Chauncey sure liked it up there; he was always taking off, going camping and so on, hunting and fishing and all. Funny, that's what I sort of thought he'd do after . . . well, after. I sort of thought he'd come back here, at least for a while. Kind of get himself together. But I don't think he ever did."

"He use to talk about it," the girl said, "but racing was in his blood. Bikes, horses, whatever. He couldn't give it up."

"Maybe." Miss Rita peered into the fog. "Wish it would clear. Really, it's so nice. But," she went on after a moment, "it seems to me that it wasn't racing exactly that was in his blood so much as it was all the stuff that went with it. The money and what it bought, and the success and what *it* bought. And when he lost it he couldn't get over the notion that it was going to happen all over again, just fall out of the sky into his lap without him really having to work at anything or stick to anything."

"He stuck with me." The girl dabbed at her nose with the Kleenex Miss Rita had given her. I got that, sugar, they can have the rest.

Miss Rita grinned. "And I bet you did everything he said, too; everything just like he wanted."

"So?"

The woman laughed out loud. "You know, I like you, kiddo. But somehow I get the notion that you're just not very bright."

The girl couldn't see what bright had to do with it. "Me and Chance didn't have to think. We just got along, that's all." She coughed, and it was like a nail, a steel icicle stabbing her right lung.

"WHAT DO YOU mean, you're going to turn him down?" Her own voice, angry and hard.

He's really drunk. The worst kind of weepy, angry, poor-me drunk, gonna pack it in, throw in the towel, people couldn't stand to see you doing good they'd try to bring you down. Florida again, but not really. That's not what's at the bottom of it. Lou French is at the bottom of it. "Sugar, who needs him? That asshole. Look how good we're doing without him."

"We're not doing good." She is astonished to hear herself say this. She has never said such a thing to him before, has never even *thought* such a thing. And if it's true, so what? They'll just pull up stakes and head on to something else. Won't they? Build that dragster, maybe, or lately he's been talking Australia—how a smart guy who didn't mind a gamble could make a fortune there in time and with a little luck. "We're not only not doing good," she goes on, "we're digging holes to bury ourself in."

"We don't need him, I tell you."

"You're not going to turn him down, Chance. I know you're not." She knows he isn't. It's just the liquor talking.

He says, "What's with you? You want to go on down there without me?" And Ellen says no, and means it. She doesn't want to go anywhere, ever, without Chance.

It's just that the place was so beautiful when she saw it that one time. The barns, the grounds, the old stone house with its gaslights and chandeliers, and the boned chicken breasts in tarragon butter (she asked), and the damask napkins (she asked about them too), and the different forks and spoons for all the different courses. She watched Lou French carefully, doing what he did and when dinner was over she had used exactly the same number of utensils as he. Chance, on the other hand, made do with the same knife and fork throughout the entire meal.

Lou French said that soon they'd have dessert—made by a different chef from the one who cooked the chicken, "though both of them are French, of course," and he smiled when Ellen laughed at his little joke. He and Chance sat there, chairs pushed back from the table, puffing big moss-green cigars, talking about everything but what was really on their minds, and then suddenly, out of the blue, Lou French turned to Ellen and said that *if* things worked out and *if* Chance came to work for him, how'd she like to go to the secretarial college that was nearby? And a little thrill of something—hope or fear, she couldn't tell—ran through her, so bright and quick and sharp that it actually hurt and she caught her breath and couldn't look at him; couldn't look at either of them, or say anything but "wow," and shake her head.

"Oh wow, I don't know." But she does know. Hasn't Mama told her? Secretaries wear pretty dresses and work in nice offices with carpets on the floor. They have lunch with their boss and get together after work, four or five of them, pretty and well-dressed, for dinner or drinks. They're worth their weight in gold, which is exactly the point Lou French is making. He has no shortage of grooms and stable girls. And he has an efficient woman who keeps the farm's books, and an accountant and a lawyer or two to keep an eye on all his various other ventures. What he doesn't have, he says, is a personal secretary. Someone to handle his correspondence and so on.

"How about it?" He smiles at her. "Interested?"

"Oh wow," like a dummy. She glances helplessly at Chance. What does he make of all this?

Chance breaks his big green cigar in half and puts one piece in his pocket for later. "Ellen's a real good little bookkeeper," he tells Lou French, "and she ain't too bad of a typer. But I sort of figured on putting her to work in the stables." He puffs at the stump of his cigar and squints at Lou French through the smoke. "I think she'll make a first-rate groom. When I get through pounding some sense into her, that is."

Lou French laughs and shoves back his chair, scraping it across the gleaming oak floor, and he slaps Chance on the shoulder. "Come on, old buddy. Let me finish showing you around the house before we have our cake."

Chance looks a little pale. Ellen wonders if she brought the Maalox. Should she tell him he better skip dessert? He'll be mad if she says anything, sick as a pack of mongrels if she doesn't. And they've been invited to stay the night. What will Lou French do if he finds out that Chance has a bad stomach? Does he know already? Will it make a difference? Before she can make up her mind Chance pushes his chair back too and follows Lou French out of the candle-lit dining room, and

Ellen has no choice but to tag along. And then, just as the three of them reach the door, Lou French turns to her and says, "Keep it in mind, young lady. I'm serious."

The main part of the house, he tells them, was completed in 1712 and was built of native stone. Other wings were added later, one in 1790 and another in 1844. He has complete records, down to the names of the workmen and the price paid for lumber and window glass. "Not a nail in the place," he says, "it's all wooden pegs," and he drops to his knees to point out the rows of peg tops in the floor of the main hall.

Soft candlelight is everywhere, glowing on the dark wood-paneled walls and the fine antique furniture selected by Lou French's wife, who is in Europe at the moment, attending an art auction. He leads them from room to room, and Ellen marvels at the rugs, the graceful chairs and tables, the portraits of his family in the study. Not photographs, real oil paintings in heavy frames. The wife, shrewd-eyed and silver-haired; two daughters, one married. "I'm a grandfather, Chance, can you believe how time flies?" The other daughter is in vet school and the son is a geologist. Ellen studies the pictures with interest, a handsome family, maybe one day she and Chance . . . And then Lou French suggests that they all step outside and get some air.

He shows them where they will live if things work out—a three-room apartment over the main barn, reached by an outside stairway. All-electric kitchen, living room with a picture window, bedroom, tile bath. It's occupied now by one of the trainers; he'll be moving out soon. However, there's no one home to let them in and show them around. Disappointed, Ellen peers through the picture window at the living room. It looks so big, the walls clean and white. And the blue carpet goes with it! She asked Lou French about that right away.

While she looks at the apartment, Chance and Lou French remain below, smoking cigars and talking. Their breath steams on the cold evening air and their voices come to her faintly. Wild stories about the Tenderloin in San Francisco where there were flophouses and greasy spoons and you had to step over the winos in the doorway on your way south to the track in the morning. "God damn," Lou French says. He seems a little drunk. They both do. "I guess it was tough," Lou French goes on, "but looking back, you know we had a good time."

Swapping lies. Ellen is happy to see the two of them joking and laughing like friends. "Do you remember," Lou French is saying as she comes down the stairs to join them, "Chance, do you remember the time up on Talking Dog Ridge when I shot the eagle?"

Ellen has heard the story at least a dozen times. Too close, too close; it always makes her uncomfortable. She tunes the men out, wondering about furniture and dishes and trying not to think about what Lou French said about secretarial school because obviously Chance doesn't like the idea and maybe Lou French didn't mean it anyway. She has never known anyone who shut the electricity off in their house on purpose. People like that aren't—can't be!—like other people. She isn't sure how far to trust him. So she concentrates on the safe things, the things that stay where you put them, dishes and plates and blue carpets, and she barely listens as Lou French reminds Chance how mad he was, how mad they all were, him and his buddies, how really disgusted, up on that ridge. Almost a week and not even a glimpse, not even a *sniff* of a deer, he says, and turns to her, drawing her in. "You should've seen our friend Chance, Ellen. Big old buck comes along, he finally gets a shot off, first one all week. And wouldn't you know!" Laughing, he puts one arm around her shoulders, rocking her a little, and she has the scary half-familiar feeling of having latched onto something swift and powerful like a river or a train. Scary, but not unpleasant. Almost nice, in fact. And if she lets go, opens her hands, it will just *take* her the way the current used to in the salt marsh years ago. It will take her, swallow her up and spit her out again, up on the bank somewhere downstream, completely changed.

She pulls away and looks at Chance. His cigar has gone out. He fumbles in his pocket for matches. Lou French laughs again. "Our friend Chance is a fine shot," he tells Ellen, "but the best shot can miss and he missed that buck by a mile."

"My sights was crooked," Chance grunts. Cigar relit, he smiles, but it's an effort.

"I never saw anyone so mad." Lou French's teeth flash as he grins. "But just then we sighted this big bird hovering up there above us, just a speck it was so high. And Chance throws his rifle down and tells me if I think I'm such a hotshot, then I should get that bird up there." He points to the sky and in spite of herself she looks up. They all do. "Chance bet me ten I couldn't do it; said it was impossible. But I made the shot." He steps back from her, hands on his hips, teeth white in his ugly-handsome face. "Biggest damn eagle you ever saw. I had that sucker stuffed and mounted," he goes on, "with the ten-dollar bill in its beak. We took it to California with us, remember, Chance?"

Still working at his smile, Chance nods.

"And remember what happened to it?"

"Aw," Chance says. "Come on, Lou. That's a long time back." But then, just as Ellen is about to remind him about the hunting lodge, he says, "Oh yeah. Took it to Frisco with us, didn't we."

"And then what?"

"Lou, what's the point . . . ?" Chance's ruddy face grows redder still. And Ellen, too, is wondering. "Oh hell," he says. "You know perfectly well we hocked it." He won't meet her eyes. He stares out across the darkening fields, his face like a slammed door. "Spent the ten and hocked the bird," and then, facing her angrily—what has *she* done?—"Now ain't that a picture? This dude," jerking his thumb at Lou French, "in a pawnshop! Slumming! Everybody's got to try the low life sometime." And then he turns from Ellen to Lou French and a look passes between the two men that she can't fathom but which makes her shiver. Uneasily she takes Chance's arm and gives it a squeeze. *Hey!* and he looks at her. At her, not through her or around her the way he's been doing, and after a moment he smiles, a little sheepishly, and smiles at Lou French too. "The good old days," he says, and Lou French agrees that indeed they were, and why don't they go on back inside now and have some dessert.

Another of his games, although of course she didn't recognize it at the time. Then later: buckaroo. Stay bought or die.

Miss Rita pointed to the south. The Double Deuce was back that way. "We passed it on the way up, but I forgot to mention it. That's Lou French's place. He raises racehorses. You probably heard Chauncey speak of him."

The girl's ears were filled with a faint crackling, like static. "Yeah," she said. "I think I heard him mention the name."

"Real nice guy. Comes out here a couple times a year, when it's deer season, and in the spring, for trout. He's got a sort of lodge-type affair way up about a thousand feet above the main part of the ranch." And she would probably have to miss his party next Tuesday, she said. First time in ages. Because of the talent scout and the trip to Vegas for her personal audition with the boss himself. "Of course it's no big deal, moneywise," she told the girl. "But Lou's parties are a lot of fun. He invites all kinds of people: everything from governors to gas station attendants. And he's an old friend, too, Lou is. I hate to disappoint him."

The girl glanced at her and then away. "That lodge of his. Is it far?"

"From here? Couple of miles as the crow flies." Anyone

could get there, Miss Rita said. Anyone, that is, that didn't mind a little mud and snow and a few rockslides. A fire trail led down from the parking lot and on over the next few ridges. "There it is." She pointed. The fog had thinned as the wind shifted, and for a moment the girl could see the trail, a faint line skating back and forth in a series of switchbacks up over the ridge on the far side of the valley.

"Is that how you get to Chance's grandmother's cabin?"

Blank stare. "What grandmother?"

"She lived up there by Copper Creek," the girl said. "You must've met her: half Indian. Paiute."

Rita continued to look baffled. "He didn't have a grandmother; it was him and his brother and his dad."

"She taught him to carve."

Rita's face cleared then and she said, "You must mean old Lenore Hensley."

"That's the one."

"But kiddo . . . she was no more Chauncey's grandmother than I am! She was just a kind of crazy old Indian, sort of a local character, you might say. After she died guys used to use her cabin as a kind of hunting camp. Maybe they still do, although I know a lot of them stay at Lou's lodge when he's not there. He leaves the door unlocked."

Sugar, this is how. . . .

Below them in the valley a narrow creek wound and flashed through the scrub and gray weeds and patches of snow. The static in the girl's ears had changed to a distant seashell-whisper. "Well," she said vaguely, watching the light fade from the creek as the fog closed in again. "Well. I guess I've taken up enough of your time. If you want to drive me on back to Cresta I'd be grateful."

Miss Rita led the way back to the car. It had been kind of fun, she remarked. Talking about Chauncey, what a character. "Why don't you come on back to my place and have a bite?"

They could continue the conversation over dinner and be in Cresta in time for the nine-thirty show. "The good old Starlite," the woman mused. She started the Mustang and put it in gear. "It's sure been good to me. I'll probably keep on doing gigs there every now and then, even after I've made it big in Vegas, just for old times' sake."

The fog was dense. Miss Rita held the car to a crawl, flicking her lights from high beam to low. The girl shivered. Her head felt strange. "How'd you and him ever end up married, anyway?"

"It was in Florida. Whoa!" as the car skidded on an icy patch. "I was down there with a band. Well, I was supposed to be with a band. This big handsome yahoo I met at the Sidewinder Club up in Sparks, he said . . . But you don't want to hear about that."

"Sure I do." They were deep in a hollow, fog like a wall reflecting the headlights as a sickly yellow glow that seemed to come from all around them and made it difficult to tell which way they were moving or if they were moving at all. The girl's stomach shifted uneasily. Both nostrils and her right ear had closed down completely and her chest hurt. She breathed carefully through her clenched teeth. The door handle she clung to was greasy with sweat.

"Well, you can guess most of it," Miss Rita said. "Of course there wasn't any band. There wasn't any anything but that yahoo and a couple of his buddies. That old story. I'd been there about six months, I guess, short on cash and trying to find gigs, and I ran into Chauncey in a bar in Miami. He'd already started to slide but you'd never have known it to see him in action. I mean, that little s.o.b. was tossing money around like it was bread crumbs and the rest of the world was birds. I should've seen it wasn't going to work."

"What happened?"

"Kiddo," reaching to adjust the heater, "he was a character

and he could be sweet when he wanted to, but he just wasn't dependable, that's all, and he let some people down. He was bound to get burned and I should've seen it coming." She leaned forward over the wheel, squinting as the road swept into a deep bend. "Everyone else did, Lord knows. It got after a while so he couldn't *buy* a ride from anyone but Lou."

"It wasn't his fault," the girl said. "He was set up."

Miss Rita shrugged. "Have it your own way."

"He was." They were coming into Boreen: comfortable-looking houses, little shops, high school, church. She said, "What really happened with that horse?"

"What horse?"

The girl sneezed. Roman candles nearly blinded her before they faded to little ashy flakes that floated in front of her eyes. "You know. When Chance lost his license."

Miss Rita pulled into a shopping center parking lot. "I'm short on o-jay," she said, "and I'm going to get you something for that cold before it turns into double pneumonia and kills you. But first I want to know what on earth you're talking about."

"I'm talking about him getting framed and the Racing Commission setting him down."

Miss Rita turned, one arm hooked over the steering wheel. "Kiddo, I guess I just don't really understand. You and me, we've got the same cast of characters, more or less, but the plot sure does differ. What's this about his license?"

The girl pressed her cheek against the cold glass of the car window. There was a movie theater at one end of the shopping center. Big bright-lit marquee: JOHN WAYNE FESTIVAL.

"You must've known about it. One of Lou's horses got disqualified. Some drug; it showed up in the saliva test. And then somebody planted a needle in Chance's glovebox and the Racing Commission took his license away."

Miss Rita tossed her hair. "Who told you that? No, never

mind, I can guess. But listen. The Racing Commission never took his license. He was a goof-off, not a crook. The worst he ever got was a week's suspension for careless riding. And as far as I recall, the only time one of Lou's horses was ever disqualified it was for bumping another horse in the stretch. There wasn't *ever* anything like a drug charge against him. Chauncey either. Take it from me."

"They yanked his license!" the girl insisted. "They did! You just forgot! So even after he left Florida he still couldn't ride. All those years. I mean, it wasn't right, because he never . . . He wouldn't! You said it yourself, he was a goof-off, not a crook! And Lou French, he was the one. I know!"

She paused, breathing hard—*watch it!* But the woman only shook her head. "Lou had nothing to do with it. Whatever happened, Chauncey brought it on himself."

The girl remained silent. After a minute or two Miss Rita said carefully, "The thing about him is he just wouldn't settle down. He really seemed to think his luck was always going to hold, no matter how much he fooled around. He was having trouble with his weight, you know, even then. Little as he was, he was big as jockeys go, but he wouldn't leave the beer alone. Fritos, french fries, all that kind of junk. Ice cream! Two o'clock in the morning and he'd haul me out of bed. Like he was pregnant or something; he just had to have a cone. And so he was spending half his life in the sweatbox and he'd come out of there weak as a cat, so it was all me and Lou and the valet together could do to get him down to the paddock by race time. But he never learned. He'd go out partying, show up late at the track the next morning. It used to drive Lou crazy but he hung with him because nobody else would, and they were friends. And then Lou caught him one time, down behind the barn doing cowboy stunts, trick roping, all kinds of crazy stuff."

"What's wrong with that?"

"Well, one of his stunts was jumping a horse over the bed of a pickup truck."

The girl nodded vigorously. A mistake. The lights of the shopping center blurred and ran together. "Well sure," she managed to say. "I've seen him do that about a hundred times."

"Not on a three-year-old colt that was entered in some big race a week later," Miss Rita said drily. "Can you imagine? About a quarter-million dollars' worth of racehorse, and there's Chauncey risking its neck just to give the grooms a thrill." Her eyes met the girl's, held briefly, slid away. "The grooms and Mrs. French. That's when Lou fired him. And that's all there was to it, kiddo. A little flirtation and a lot of irresponsibility. Take it from me."

It didn't make sense. Well, the horse part, yes. She could see him doing that, lost in the moment the way he'd get sometimes. Probably one of the grooms bet he couldn't do it. "Put your money where your mouth is," Chance would say, and his obligations to Lou French, the horse's upcoming race—none of that would have mattered. Yes, she could see it. That was the way he was. Had been. But Mrs. French? The boss's wife, that stern-eyed lady? That too, she supposed. It was the sort of thing he just might have tried, just once, just to see what would happen. She folded her arms. Her breath rattled in her lungs. "What else?"

Miss Rita said carefully, "Even when Chauncey was doing good he wasn't doing *so* good, if you follow. He couldn't handle it. He had that one big year when he won all those races and it went to his head, I guess." She paused, fingers drumming lightly on the wheel. "The way most people saw it, Lou had no real call to keep him on as long as he did. But Lou's a good-hearted guy and he's loyal. He could see what was happening with Chauncey and he'd still go on and give him another shot."

"That's for damn sure," the girl said bitterly. "Right in the head."

Miss Rita's hand lay still on the steering wheel. She studied the girl's face, the puzzlement in her eyes slowly giving way to shock and anger. "So that's what you think."

"No think to it," the girl said. "I know for a rockbound fact." Miss Rita was wrong or lying, one or the other, just as Bucky Rowe had been wrong or lying and Chance had been wrong and she herself, all of them taken in by his money and his smile and that ability he had to look right inside you and pull out things you didn't even know were there. Make you an offer you couldn't refuse. Out of the salt marsh and onto solid ground. Buy into the partnership; secretarial school. She knew for a certainty, without having to ask, that somewhere along the line Lou French had helped Miss Rita in some way with her singing career, and Bucky with his piece of the Golden Starlite. He'd bought them all, and Bucky and Miss Rita had stayed bought and Chance hadn't and that was the difference.

Miss Rita removed her arm from the wheel and flexed her elbow, shaking her hand as if it had gone to sleep. "I can see you really got it in for Lou," she said, "and I guess that's your business. All I know is Lou did everything a man could be expected to do under the circumstances, and then some. He hung with Chauncey through all kinds of trouble, and then when things got *so* rough, he still gave him rides when he could, and talked him up to his friends, and meanwhile what's Chauncey doing but playing the fool. Driving drunk; speed to make the weight, rainbows to get down off the speed. My God, that stupid accident. . . ."

"When the Buick fell off the jack?"

Miss Rita nodded. "The reason it fell off the jack was he was so wasted he forgot to set the brake. And then Mrs. French . . ." She glanced at the girl, reached over and touched her arm. "I'm sorry. I can see how you felt about him, and maybe he changed by the time you knew him. Maybe he straightened out some. Probably he did; I hope so, anyway.

But you asked me how it was when *I* knew him, and that's what I'm telling you."

"Sure," the girl said. "I understand."

Cold air struck her as Miss Rita opened the car door. "Hang in there, kiddo." She knew the druggist, she'd bring back a little something for that cough.

9

ONCE WHEN it was snowing he borrowed a camera from someone because he'd heard you could take pictures of the flakes. Crazy, she said, it would never work, but he shushed her—"trust me, sugar"—and fussed happily for hours it seemed, setting up the lights and the reflectors just so, excited as a kid. Camera on a special stand placed on the table in the Airstream's galley, door propped open, as cold inside as out and what we need's black velvet, sugar. "Come on, where's that fancy skirt of yours?"

A beautiful skirt, never worn. Bought for some party they didn't go to. She can't remember why and has the dark feeling that maybe this is for the best, that maybe he was too drunk to drive or that he'd decided at the last minute he'd rather go up to Pennsylvania with Ray Vincent for the opening day of deer season, that maybe it had been graduation night all over again. At any rate, the skirt has been on its hanger ever since, and although she has taken it from the closet a time or two, just looking, just because it's pretty, she has never put it on. It's special, for a special occasion, maybe for that trip to Florida, to Fort Lauderdale and Disney World. "Come on," Chance says. "Sugar, I really need it."

It's not real velvet, but that makes no nevermind, he says. "It's perfect. Just cut me off a piece."

She stares at him. "What?"

"Sugar! Don't give me no grief!" He's at the door, dancing with impatience. Bundled in his jacket and cap, gazing expectantly up at the sky, he looks oddly vulnerable and innocent, a too-big child. And she remembers or thinks she remembers— it might have been a dream—standing at the top of a long hill somewhere, she and Jimmy Lee, the road dipping away before them, newly paved and white without a rut or chuckhole anywhere, no traffic, no parked cars and not another soul in sight. Just her and him and that road dipping straight and smooth, unwinding like a ball of string as far as she could see. Smooth and straight, no traffic, no taunting kids, no midnight moves, no strange men in the bathroom in the morning. It's the Getaway Road; it's all downhill. The wagon will roll by itself, they both can ride.

Or she can ride alone. Leave Jimmy and just go.

"How big a piece you want?" she asks, and uses the kitchen shears to cut a square the size he indicates. She watches him stretch the cloth taut between his hands and step outside. Giant flakes drift gently down—a pretty, pretty snow. Chance holds out the velvet. A soft flake settles and he turns, smiling at her and sliding the black cloth quickly into place beneath the camera's lens. "Take a look at this."

Crazy, she says, but she can't stay mad, not even about the skirt—she'd probably never have worn it anyhow. And there's no point in trying to reason with him when he's caught up in something this way. She bends over the viewfinder and closes her left eye. The flake is huge. It fills her vision, seeming to jump at her, sparkling like sugar and perfect as a star. Then as she watches, its edges soften and begin to slide and blur. She blinks. When she looks again a shiny bead of water stands where the flake had been, but never mind, he says. Arm around her shoulders, he leads her to the door. "Look at it come down! We're snowflake millionaires! Here," handing her the velvet. "Go ahead, it's on the house! Take any one you want."

The pictures come back from the developer within a week. Chance tapes them all, the entire dozen, to the galley wall, so proud he can't even wait for her to make a regular display for them, with mat board and a frame. "Hey sugar, maybe I ought to quit the bikes; go into the photography business!" And, truly, the prints are beautiful. Like spun-sugar doilies, she thinks, but secretly she prefers the negatives. Hold them to the light and see black snowflakes on a yellow-white ground. She can't say why they fascinate her so, and Chance sees nothing special about them—"sugar, you just like things bass-ackwards, that's all"—but they do. She waits until he's off somewhere else so he won't laugh and then looks at them, sometimes for an hour or more; she loses track of time. *Black* snowflakes. No such thing but there they are. Like inside-out explosions, she tells herself, or the backsides of stars.

"Of course I've got pictures," Rita said. "He was a real slice of ham, that boy. I've got a bunch somewhere in an old album. Fix me a drink, kiddo, I'll hunt it up for you." And off she went, leaving the girl to slop gin into a glass, scrounge in the freezer for a tray of ice, curse when it stuck to her fingers. No solid ground. No solid anything, black snowflakes with no more substance than the wind; not half the substance of Miss Rita's voice calling, "Hey! Found it! What about that drink?"

The album was in the dresser in the bedroom, in a lower drawer filled with scraps and trinkets and spools of thread. Rubber bands, shoehorn, key ring with a big green plastic tag:

SPARES. The bedroom itself was really nice. Crisp white curtains. A white flounce peeped from beneath the yellow-flowered bedspread. The carpet was the kind you had to vacuum with a special attachment. A shag rake, it was called. The girl had seen one demonstrated in the big new Sears in Scott's Run. Miss Rita opened the album and began plucking out snapshots, an even half dozen in all. Four from Florida, one from New Orleans, she said, and one from his fairground days.

The girl fanned the photos like a poker hand so that she could see them all at once. So strange. A boy—a *kid*, younger than she was now—stared up at her, from a beach blanket, from in front of a palm tree, from the back of a sleek racehorse, from behind the wheel of a red convertible. He had a white smile, dark blond hair worn long, and he was no one she really knew. Somebody she might have met; somebody she'd seen around. She carried the pictures with her to the kitchen and studied them while Miss Rita fried hamburgers, warmed rolls, opened a can of cream-style corn. Finally she said, "I don't guess you knew Lou French had hired him on again."

"He did?" Mildly, tasting the corn, reaching for the pepper shaker. "Well, Chauncey could ride, no doubt about that. I guess Lou thought it was worth taking another chance." And when the girl didn't answer, "Lou's like that, that's all. He'll help you out. After Chauncey and me split up the first time he offered to pay my way to Nashville with no strings attached, just so I could start over and make something of my life. Just out of the goodness of his heart. Of course I couldn't accept something like that, but you have to admit it was nice."

"Very nice," the girl agreed, wondering what all that niceness had bought. Not sex. Not just sex, anyway. She figured he could have had that for free. "Where's the silver at?" she asked. "I'll set the table."

"Left of the stove. Mats and napkins down below. I know you don't like Lou," Miss Rita went on, "and maybe he gave you good reason. But let me tell you this: you're all by yourself on that one, if it's true." She turned from the stove, cheeks flushed, one hand in a green and white oven mitt, to face the girl. "I've known him a long time, and he was never anything but decent. Not just to me, but to everyone I know of. Of course," bending to pull the rolls from the oven, "there's always jealousy when somebody's as successful as Lou. He started out from nothing, you know, just like Chauncey did. No family to speak of, worked in the copper mines in Tonopah when he was just a kid, did a little rodeoing and horse breaking on the side. And then he showed up here, at the fairgrounds track, with some broken-down horse he'd claimed up in Canada somewhere."

"Bull!" Miss Rita's druggist-friend's cough syrup worked like a champ. Codeine, the label said. The girl's ears had cleared; her sore throat had retreated to a single small scratchy area that didn't hurt unless she swallowed. Her mind ran clear and cold as a high-country stream, so that she could see things in a cold clear way. Right now, for example, she could see how important it was that she set Miss Rita straight. "When he got to the fairgrounds he was already rich," she explained as the woman set a plate before her. "For all I know he was born rich. Showed up at the track one morning riding in a red and silver van about the size of a 747 airplane, and he had this colored driver in a general's uniform, and all new tack and equipment and three good horses. All he needed was somebody to ride for him, and he chose Chance. Picked him right out of the bunch, and that's how it was. Anybody tells you different, then they're lying."

"That how he told it?" Miss Rita asked, and the girl could hear, with her newly cleared ears, a cube of ice going tink, tink, against the sides of the glass and even the tiny private whisper of sloshing juice.

"That's how it was."

The ice tinked in the glass, knocked with a woodier sound against the woman's teeth as she drank, swallowing with something almost like a thud. The girl was surprised not to be able to hear the liquid's progress down Miss Rita's throat, the splash as it dropped into her stomach—like water gurgling in the exposed overhead gutters in the Quonset hut before it spilled into the cistern. Miss Rita set her glass down, almost empty, and wiped her mouth carefully on a paper napkin. "Okay," she said. "That's how it was."

She didn't believe it for a minute; the girl knew that, and it was okay. Unimportant. Miss Rita was in Lou French's pocket, and that was okay too. It didn't matter. Chance was what mattered, all the missing pieces that Miss Rita had squirreled away. First things first. Find him and then go on.

They finished the meal in silence, washed up, and then it was time for Miss Rita to shower and dress for the evening's show. The girl followed her to the bedroom, sat down carefully so as not to rumple the flowered spread and watched as Miss Rita set out her costume. Maroon pants this time, and a pink shirt with sequins; her white hat had a beaded Indian band. "Did I understand you right?" she asked. "Were you and Chance married, and then you separated and got back together?"

"Right." Miss Rita threaded a beaded belt through the waist loops on the maroon pants. "He kind of bailed me out in Miami that time, and we were together—got married and were together, I'd had it up to here with fooling around—for oh, maybe a year, year and a half. And then he had that trouble and Lou had to set him down, and then he took off. That was when Lou was going to send me to Nashville, but I couldn't let him do that, you know. And anyhow, I was doing okay there in Miami by that time, getting gigs and all; there was even a guy talking record contract, like *he* was going to send me to Nashville. But then Chauncey showed up again and he swore he was straight, had a steady job at a gas station not so far from New Orleans that I couldn't find work there if I wanted, at the clubs.

"To tell the truth," trying silk scarves—white, red, then purple—against the pink shirt, "which one d'you like? To tell you the truth," before the girl could answer, "I'd found myself in a little bit of a pickle; the record contract guy had some pretty sleazy friends, drug dealers and pimps, and I wasn't sorry to be getting out of Miami for a while. And Chauncey, well, you know he could be sweet when he wanted, and I guess I thought maybe we could work things out." She smiled. "Nobody'd have been any happier than me if we could've. But Chauncey never was one for working things out, was he? He wasn't straight, and the so-called steady job was about as steady as a drunk on a tightrope, I mean it was just one thing and then another, and after the baby came he just laid down his load and walked."

"Wait a minute!" Wife. Kid. *You and me, sugar.* The girl watched in the dressing table mirror as Miss Rita removed the trees from her tall black and red boots. Okay. Anybody could get divorced, just look in the newspapers. But nobody, at least nobody like Chance, would leave a kid. Would they? *Take him to the fairgrounds, show him where his old man got his start.* Oh Jesus God. Stale perfume-smelling air rushed through her newly cleared nose, burning her newly drained sinuses. She asked evenly, "How old's he now? Six? Seven?"

Miss Rita moved to her chest of drawers. Black bra and panties. "The baby had a bad heart," she said. "Born that way. They operated, but it didn't help." Sheer knee-length stockings, a mismatched pair. She put one back, selected another. "I never even brought him home from the hospital; I never even held him but twice. He was in one of those isolettes, and, oh, there was a lot of flu going around, and some kind of strep. We took back the crib and stuff to the department store, and then it was almost like he never was."

"I'm sorry," the girl said. "Christ."

"No use to be. It was a long time ago." The woman studied the stockings in her hand. "Thomas."

"What?"

"That was his name. After Chauncey's father. And then Chauncey walked, and that was the last I saw of him for almost seven years, until last December when his father passed away." Miss Rita draped the stockings over the tops of her boots. "How about you, kiddo? You got a family?"

"Not much of a one." The girl shrugged. "My parents weren't married; my mom hooked up with this preacher," thinking of white shoes, a white dress: *bretheren and sisteren I have truly seen the light.* Thinking that maybe for about one minute and a half, just maybe she truly had. She and Mama both, on that trip to Nashville. A missed bus connection somewhere in Alabama; too late for the Reverend Joe Michael Simms's televised revival but they did catch another tent meeting that had just come to town. Not to town, really, not actually to Nashville, but to the outskirts. And Brother Hosea was a Texas boy from Vista Sol, just twelve miles from Galveston. And didn't he look like Jesus? Mama said. That beard, those eyes. "Lambie, it was God's own sweet will that brought us to this man."

THE PRETTY blond woman makes lists, order where there is none; the little girl connects her numbered dots. Do it right, make no mistakes, and Jimmy Lee will be like other kids and Daddy will come home. A ship's captain, so handsome in his uniform. She really did believe that—all of it—for a while. Deals and signs, that strange and ancient *something* rising out of the channel to regard her with its rheumy eye. Knothole.

Nail head. None of it meant anything. Things were how things were and you made the best of them, and when the men left and the money ran out you put your brother in his little cart and dragged him to the landlord and you smiled and said please, could he wait another week?

And then you turn thirteen and then fourteen, and even if you aren't pretty guys start to follow you home. And then one day Mama tells you maybe you ought to leave Jimmy Lee behind next time. Go on down and see Mr. Portillo.

"What for, Mama? Rent's not due."

"Wear this." One of her own pretty dresses. Cut low. "Just go on down and talk to him, lambie. That's all, just talk to the man. Be nice to him."

Lord knows where it might have ended. The girl supposed she had Hosea to thank for one thing, at least.

"Strange and wonderous are the ways and workings of the Lord," Brother Hosea said. His voice filled the tent and people fell down on their knees. Mama did, and Ellen did too, although she'd told herself beforehand that she wasn't going to, that it was all a trick; that she'd already been fooled enough times, out there in the salt marsh, seeing devils in floating rotten logs and waiting for signs to fall out of the sky. But she knew better now. You'd have to *really* be a fool to let yourself be taken in again. But when Hosea said, "Kneel!" down she went.

Strange and wondrous. The ways and workings of the Lord. That night in the motel room she tells herself that in this case at least it might be true. Because they're here in Nashville, the three of them seeking a miracle, as the direct result of Mama's attack on a sailor in some Galveston waterfront bar. Maybe, Mama had said afterward, it was the uniform, or something about his voice. The way he moved in the uncertain light. A broken bottle; she smashed it herself on the edge of the bar and went for his eyes. He pushed her away. "Lambie, he *laughed* at me!" And when she came at him again he broke her nose. A draw, the bar regulars agreed; a good show, no need to call the cops. But Mama was scared. "Lambie, I'd have killed him if I could. Your daddy. I thought he was your daddy, the one true love of my life, and I'd have killed him." That was when she started watching the revivals on TV, and *that* was when she learned about the Reverend Joe Michael Simms, who could make the blind to see and the lame to walk. Maybe—it was actually Ellen's suggestion, although she didn't believe for a minute that it was really possible—he could also make the slow to think. She was almost joking, just telling Mama what Mama wanted to hear, but then in that Nashville motel after listening to Brother Hosea preach . . . It was really strange. There for a minute he'd had her going too. Without even touching her, without even coming near, he'd managed to take hold of her and there she was. Down there on her knees with all the rest.

She looks at Jimmy Lee, sitting where she left him on the bed, his face turned toward the snow-filled TV screen. He's sixteen now but people take him for eight or nine, he's that small. But Ellen helps him dress and use the toilet and she knows that in some ways at least he's almost a grown man. Mama knows it too; says, "Lambie, maybe you shouldn't ought to spend quite so much time . . ." but that's all she says. If Ellen doesn't stay with Jimmy, *she'll* have to.

Ellen looks at him there on the bed, staring at the TV screen. His mouth is open. Wet. Smiling. Snow or picture makes no nevermind to him; TV's TV and he likes it all. She watches him for a minute or so and thinks, no. Hosea can preach till he's blue in the face, but as for helping Jimmy, as for any miracle at all—forget it!

The girl said, "I just don't think I was cut out to live in the same house with a preacher."

Miss Rita nodded. Preachers could be hard.

"Harder than me by a long shot." She looked down at her hands pressed together between her knees. They seemed enormously far away, her arms swooping down to them like cables. "See, Hosea was going to cure my brother Jimmy of being retarded. It was going to be a miracle. And, well, me and Hosea didn't get along and he said I was keeping it from working, and then some things happened, and," with a small shrug, "Mama kicked me out."

Kicked out by your own mother—that was tough, Miss Rita said, and the girl said yeah, it was tough.

"You ever try going back?"

"Nope."

But she had, once. A year ago August she and Chance had gone to Baton Rouge, where Chance was supposed to connect up with somebody who had a line on some Japanese bikes that might come in cheap by way of Mexico. It was hot in Louisiana and Chance had his mind on other things. The bike deal didn't look too good, up close, but he'd run into three or four other guys he knew from somewhere; he was having a great time playing cards, swapping tales; he had other irons in other fires, he said. He'd get along just fine without her for a day or two. Sure, sugar, go see your folks if you want. She wasn't sure she *wanted* to—want didn't seem to have much to do with it. But to be so close. She didn't understand it, but she wondered how they were doing, Mama and Jimmy Lee.

The house looked just the same. It still needed paint and there was still an old car—a different one, but not too different—parked slaunchwise by the porch, one front corner jacked up and the tire and wheel and some rusty tools lying in the weeds beside it.

Late evening. Frogs in the culvert and locusts singing in the trees. Swallows heading for home; bats darting and mosquitoes and no-see-ums. The Gulf is close; you can smell it, and all three of them are sitting there on the old red glider on the porch.

The glider squeaks and the gate slumps open when she unhooks the latch. Mama says, "Oh, Ellie-lamb!" and Ellen's heart leaps with relief. She's been forgiven!

Her mother's face is plain and lined now, with no makeup. House slippers, a flowered dress; she's put on weight. She starts to get up from the glider but Hosea lifts his hand. He could almost be blessing her. It's that kind of gesture, but that's not what he's doing. "Sit still," he says. And to Ellen, sharply, "What *you* want?"

He has shaved off his beard and no longer looks the least bit like Jesus. His chin recedes, his upper lip's a beak, her mother's hair is gray. Ellen herself is almost slim now, her hair short and curled the way Chance likes it; she wears a pretty blouse. Only Jimmy hasn't changed. Jimmy will never change. He sits beside their mother, patting himself, jiggling his foot, head bobbing on his reedy neck. She watches him for a moment. Disneyland.

"Come crawlin' back, did you?" Hosea says. "I hope you ain't pregnant."

The moon comes up yolk-orange, so full and heavy that you'd think it would peel right off the sky. Or burst with a splash, drenching the dunes and the salt marsh. The Gulf shines up at them, green-black and flecked with foam. Low tide; it seems to have drawn in on itself, contracting and relaxing like a muscle under its gleaming glassy hide.

Mama's white dress glows green as water in the moonlight. She says, "Lambie, you know we can't."

"Why not?"

Because they just can't. Her and Jimmy Lee. Just up and leave; fly in the face of God's will and go back to West Virginia with Ellen.

They sit on a mossy stone at the end of the jetty. Mama takes off her shoes. Sneakers, now. Not sandals, not high-heeled sandals, not anymore. She cools her feet in the water. Insect repellent instead of My Sin.

"It's not what you think, Mama. I love him."

It's surprising how much light the moon sheds. Ellen can see her mother's feet in the water, the green waves wrinkling around her ankles. Her feet, pale and delicate, bend off from her legs at broken-looking angles. She says, "Ellie, I'm just not strong enough. Do you hear what I'm saying?"

Ellen hears nothing but the Gulf—a fish smacking the surface, the near-yet-distant hissing of the waves—and the cackling cry of some night-hunting bird. "I graduated high school!" she tells her mother. It's an odd thing to say, and afterward she wonders about it. "We can find a bigger place." She wonders about this too. Give up the Airstream? "We'll work out a way!"

Her mother shakes her head. In the moonlight her hair is blond again. "I know you don't like him, lambie. I know you don't believe. But even if it isn't God's will it's worked out pretty good. He treats me okay and he looks after Jimmy, and," with a smile, "you never did like okra neither, as I recall."

They sit there for a while, close together in the moon-filled silence, and then Mama says, "It's not what you think, either. Love don't change it, lambie. Love don't change a God damn thing."

THE GIRL sat carefully on the yellow bedspread, studying the heavy ornate lines of the tallboy chest, the dressing table's white ruffled skirt, the gold-framed mirror and pictures. It must have cost a bundle. Really, it was straight out of *House Beautiful*. A broken-down singer like Miss Rita . . . where had she come up with that kind of money?

No problem, she supposed, if you were in Lou French's pocket. No sign of any other man. But there were men who left no sign; nothing personal like a toothbrush that could tie them to you. Talent scouts, she thought, and managers of sleazy nightclubs. Sailors, captains on cruise ships, the not-so-fancy ones that left from Galveston instead of Houston. Guys like that, they'd pass through your life, throw you a few crumbs—take you to the movies, get you pregnant, maybe a few bucks toward the rent. But when push came to shove it was lambie, *you* go. With or without Jimmy, because the man had passed on through like all the others and all that was left was a commemorative vahz or a busted nose or a wish or a dream and Chance was the end of all that. Chance was real. He had been real. She touched the wooden horse head where it lay in the hollow of her throat. His signs were everywhere. It was just that she was no longer sure how to read them.

"Looks nice, don't you think?" Miss Rita had finished laying out her costume on the chair beside the bathroom door. Pink shirt, maroon pants, blood red scarf for her neck. The white hat perched on the back of the chair above the shirt, boots tall and stiff nearby. She stepped back, admiring the effect, draping the white gun belt with its silly holster and pistol across the pants on the chair's seat.

The little revolver looked surprisingly real. There was something about the way the woman handled it, and about the way the holster swung before she set it down, as if there was a solidness, real weight. The girl could almost feel it dragging like a current against her own arm as she tried to lift it, hold it steady, fire. She cleared her throat. "I guess that's just a toy."

Oh no, Miss Rita said indignantly. It was real. Real and legal and licensed. "I've got bullets for it too," she said. "Living alone like I do, you have to be prepared. Of course, it's not

loaded when I wear it onstage." And then, frowning, she
turned to the girl and asked, "Do you think it's maybe just a
little melodramatic? I mean for tonight, with that guy coming
and all? Do you think it might look just a little tacky?" Before
the girl could make up her mind, Miss Rita had tossed the
gun and holster onto the bed. "Definitely too flashy. I think
this guy wants something more sincere. And Lord! would you
look at the time!" She'd better get a wiggle on; she still had to
set her hair and do her nails. She held out her glass to the
girl. "Make me another one of these, would you, and then
come talk to me while I shower."

"What now?" Miss Rita yelled over the noise of the water.
"You came here to find out about him and you've found out,
and where do you go from here?"

The girl sat on the toilet seat and watched steam roll up
over the fish-and-seahorse curtain, condensing and running
down the walls and mirror while Rita's shadow lathered its
head and soaped its crotch and armpits and sang in Rita's
lonesome voice little snatches of Rita's songs:

> *How many times have you heard someone say*
> *If I had his money, I could do things my way*
> *But little they know that it's so hard to find*
> *One rich man in a hundred with a satisfied mind*

The singing stopped abruptly. "Did you hear what I said? I
said what are your plans now? And hand me a towel, would
you, kiddo?"

The girl handed her a towel. "Oh, I got a job lined up."

"What doing?" Miss Rita flung back the curtain and stepped
out, towel more or less about her waist. Slack breasts, white-
laddered abdomen; she wiped a circle in the fogged mirror.

"Bookkeeper. A trucking firm in California."

The woman opened her mouth and drew her lips back, examining teeth and gums, reaching for the dental floss. "That doesn't sound very fascinating."

The girl shrugged.

"That what you want to do, be a bookkeeper?"

"What I wanted to do was be with Chance."

Miss Rita turned slowly to face her. "Chauncey's dead. I asked, do you want to be a bookkeeper?"

"Well," sulkily, "bookkeeping's okay. It's a job, and I've done it before. The truth is, I don't really care."

Miss Rita leaned close to the mirror, scrutinizing her teeth again. Then, apparently satisfied, "Kiddo, you're really something else, you know that? Here you are . . . what? eighteen years old?"

"Twenty," picking at the nap of a washcloth. "Almost." As if any of this mattered. Her throat had started to hurt again and she had to be careful not to breathe too deeply. The bathroom seemed terribly warm.

"Okay, so you're twenty, and you've rolled over and pointed your toes to the sky. You think you're the first person whose boyfriend ever died?"

A blue washcloth. Little white flowers on the border. Nice clothes, nice office, lunch with the boss. She said, "I don't care."

Miss Rita gave her a look that would have split a stone. "You've got your whole damn *life* left in front of you! Look at me . . . look careful!" Red-rimmed eyes, wrinkled lids and gullied cheeks. This close, the part in her damp hair showed a sixteenth-inch of gray. "Do you want to end up like me? I could have made it! I could have gone to Nashville!"

"But you said circumstances. . . ."

Miss Rita shook her head. "I could have gone; I could have ·

worked out a way—let Lou send me. Probably he meant it about no strings. But even if he didn't, I wouldn't be the first girl who traveled on her back to where she wanted to go, now would I? And same goes for that other guy. If I'd wanted it bad enough, knew how bad I'd want it now . . . I should have gone," she said. "I should have at least tried."

The girl said hesitantly, "The talent scout?"

"Yeah, there's him. But look at me," dismissing herself with a little brushing motion of one hand. "I know I can still sing— well, hell, you've heard me. But kiddo, I'm forty-two years old. You figure it out. If there really is a club you know what it'll be like. Not on the Strip, you bet your bones. Off in some dark alley: the Last Chance Saloon."

"So why even go through with it?" the girl asked. "You're doing okay here."

The woman's eyes glittered. "Because it *might* not be like that! It *might* be real! Kiddo, this is it for me, I can't say no." She paused, clutching the towel to her waist. "Just one break, that's all I need and I'll be on my way again. I'll cut a record; it'll be a hit, you know it will, you've heard me! And youth's not everything. Look at all the mature girls who've been stars. Marlene Dietrich, Mae West, it's talent that counts! Talent and intestinal fortitude and the breaks. I've got the first two, all I need's the last." She looked at the girl and nodded sharply. "Go ahead. Be a bookkeeper. If that's what you really want to do."

The steamy room reeled as the girl got slowly to her feet. Her bad knee threatened to buckle; she steadied herself with one hand on the towel rack. "Would you drop it? I tell you, I don't care." Poor Rita, she thought dully as she limped from the bathroom. Poor Rita, who wasn't going to Vegas. Who wasn't going anywhere.

From where she stood she could just see the woman through

the bathroom door; just her shoulder and one arm, and one hip draped in the yellow towel. She was rolling her hair on a hot-curler, her face in the mirror closed and intent. The girl glanced at the pistol on the bed, wondered briefly where the bullets for it were, and then moved silently across the room to the chest of drawers.

Scraps, trinkets, spools of thread; rubber bands, shoehorn, and yes, a box of cartridges. There were four keys on the ring with the big plastic tag. Two looked like house keys, one was maybe for a suitcase. The fourth said Ford Motor Company. Breathing carefully through clenched teeth, she unsnapped the tag from the ring, slipped the keys into her pocket and closed the drawer. She had no idea why. Five minutes later, Miss Rita found her in the kitchen, shakily measuring out another spoonful of medicine.

By the time they returned to Cresta her lungs were on fire and she was coughing again in spite of the codeine. Hot shower, she promised herself, double handful of aspirin, wash it all down with another slug of that syrup. But first, Miss Rita said, why didn't she come by the Starlite, meet the band, meet the talent scout, "I sure wish you'd reconsider and let me buy you a drink." And the girl, breathing carefully through her teeth, thought, Why not? Alcohol to kill the germs. Medicinal purposes. Splash of this, little dab of that; honey, lemon, good for what ails you. Roses in your cheeks, hair on your chest, starch in your spine. Chance used to say that. Starch in your pecker. He used to say that too. And, name your poison.

"Wild Turkey," she said to Miss Rita. "On the rocks."

The guys in the band had names—Phil, Ron, Dean and Bobby—but she couldn't keep them straight. The whiskey had gone to her head. And any germs it had killed must have been for tomorrow's disease; she still felt terrible. Booze and dope. She'd have laughed if she dared. T-for-trouble. On the road again. "I better take off," she tried to tell Miss Rita, "before I go flat on my face," but her voice didn't work right and anyway Miss Rita was talking to someone else. The girl finished her drink and slid shakily down from her stool.

Outside it was bitterly cold. Still, she stopped off at the Texaco on her way back to the hotel. The only pay phone at the Aberdeen was right there on the wall in the lobby. The gas station booth at least was private. And it had a phone book, hanging by a chain.

His phone rang and rang and rang. Finally he answered. "Rumstead."

Silence. What to say? She sneezed, hot orange fading to violet, and he said, "Bless you." Friendly guy, those acne-scarred cheeks, maybe that was it. She had liked him. She remembered that. And he was a farrier, a horseshoer. Somehow she knew without having to ask that one of the places he worked would have to be the Double Deuce. "My name," she said, struggling with a tongue that felt stiff as the clapper of a bell, "is . . ." She almost said Helen, almost went on with the act, but what came out was her own true name. "Ellen Flint. From Galveston, Texas. Met you inna Crossroads th'other morning."

That's how it sounded to her but he seemed to understand perfectly. And yes, he remembered. She had been looking for a friend, hadn't she? "Ever find him?"

"Not yet."

The wires hummed. She concentrated on taking shallow breaths. "Well," he said after a moment, "I'm sorry, but I really don't see what else. . . ."

She had liked him. Not just liked him but found him attractive, scarred cheeks and all. And he had liked her. Of course he hadn't said so but she knew. Something she'd figured was dead forever came to life with a rush and she said, "Gene?"

"Yes?"

"I didn't exactly call about that." She shivered. Reaching into her purse for the bottle of cough syrup, she uncapped it, took a swig and then another. If a little was good, a little more was bound to be better. If it wasn't Lou French it was the Eustices, just bad luck. Gene Rumstead could tell her about Sun River if anyone could, and one way or the other she needed to know. One last swallow for luck, and one last lie. "My friend used to be a jockey but he's a breeder now. And there was this horse he wanted to buy. A broodmare; a chestnut Thoroughbred. It was at the Double Deuce and then it disappeared."

"That must've been June O'Meara's horse," he told her after a moment's thought. "Pretty Penny. She's a barrel racer, though; a gymkhana horse, not a broodmare. She went lame last fall and June turned her out for a while to rest." The O'Mearas were friends of the Frenches; that was why the horse had been at Lou's ranch. Yes, he was sure. And yes, he knew where—exactly where, for that matter—the animal was now. "Blue Sky Stables, out near Iron Springs. June's got her back in training. I put shoes on her last week."

And that was that. Ellen wasn't really surprised. Lou French, that rich, respected man, that up-by-his-bootstraps Nevada buckaroo who hadn't forgotten his friends, who hunted deer with gas station attendants and guys from the Feed and Seed as well as congressmen and brain surgeons . . . He wasn't selling ringers and he hadn't had Chance killed.

Two poor drunk country boys rolling dice, just bad luck, no meaning to it, life was just a crapshoot after all. Damn you, Chance, she thought. Damn you, *why? Why lie to me?* Thinking that if he were to come back to life, if he were to appear before her now, this instant, in the flesh, she'd probably kill him herself, with her bare hands. Damn you, Chance. That wasn't right!

But her anger didn't last; it faded quickly, as feeble as her legs as she made her way haltingly back to the Aberdeen. Damn you, Chance, she thought, but the edge was gone; damn them all, whoever they all were. It hardly seemed to matter. Lou French? Not his jet, the fat man says. Smart as he is . . . took him to the cleaners. And the fat man's friend: I hear . . . hock his granny. Selling off his breeding stock.

My wife says I care more about those mares and foals than I do about her. Just kidding, of course.

So that was it. That was what you got when you did business with A-rabs. She believed that was it; there was no doubt at all in her mind. Taken to the cleaners, that rich and clever man. By the time she reached the hotel steps her anger had all but disappeared, numbed out and replaced by something that she recognized dimly as relief.

We're all of us killers. Maybe so. But it all came down to where you drew the line, and hers had been erased. Wiped clean. She didn't have to shoot anyone. She could be on the bus west tomorrow. No more trouble; make T-for-Turlock by 9 p.m. Bookkeeping wasn't so bad. And maybe there'd be a secretarial school near there somewhere. Maybe she could go part time, maybe work in that nice office someday after all. Maybe she'd come back to Cresta on vacation. Maybe she'd see Gene Rumstead again.

It was a good plan. She liked it, and the sooner she got started carrying it out the better. But first things first, and she could barely climb the steps to the front door. She staggered into the lobby and collapsed into a chair behind a dusty plastic fern and just sat there while the floor bucked and heaved beneath her, trying to work up the energy and ambition to walk the rest of the way across the room to the stairs. Hey, she thought without much interest, you really are sick. You could die. Right here in this chair in the lobby behind the fern.

"Hey," she said or thought she said to the night clerk.

Maybe if he'd help her upstairs? Or maybe he could call a doctor. But the clerk was busy. A man stood at the desk, leaning over the register, speaking in a voice too low for her to hear. A big guy, shoulders like haunches of beef beneath the khaki jacket. The girl saw the clerk shrug. She saw a key change hands. She shrank down to nothing in her chair, holding her breath as the county sheriff gave the night clerk a businesslike nod and strode across the lobby toward the stairs.

So what did it prove? Absolutely nothing; she knew that. The Aberdeen was hardly the Holiday Inn. All kinds of people stayed there. She'd seen them, and some of them you wouldn't want to touch without a pair of rubber gloves. But they weren't the reason the sheriff was here. Lou French was the reason; Lou French and his people with their ears to the ground. They'd found her out. Just as she was leaving, just as she'd given up, let herself be fooled. . . . She should have known; should have picked it up some way—a feeling like the close, charged stillness in the air before a storm. Gene Rumstead, nice Gene Rumstead, attractive Gene Rumstead that friendly faced cowboy of a horseshoer, was in Lou French's pocket too, with all the others. Very likely it was he who had called the sheriff. He'd have just about had time. *Sugar, they'll set you up, and then they'll set you down.* She couldn't believe she'd doubted him, even for a minute.

The sheriff was probably searching her room by now. She could almost see him testing the air—sniffing, poking out his tongue like a snake, tasting to see if she'd been there, tasting for danger. He would bring his own scent with him: a mustiness, like a cage in which an animal used to live. And now she could almost see him opening her suitcase, pawing among the bottles and tubes of makeup on the dresser, looking with interest at the box of maxipads, which is far too heavy for its advertised contents. Cool and professional, he reaches inside. His fingers close around the barrel of the gun. He feels the bag of cartridges. Satisfied, he sits down on the bed to wait.

Judging by the parking lot, there's a good crowd in the Golden Starlite for the nine-thirty show. Ellen runs her hand along the front fender of a long black Lincoln. The talent scout, she thinks. Poor Rita. The Last Chance Saloon. Taking the spare keys from her purse, she fits the square-ended Ford Motor Company one into the pink Mustang's lock. Damn! she thinks. I never stole a car before.

But it's easy. You just get in and drive away.

10

ROUTE 212 snakes uphill, mostly clear of snow but wet. Yellow reflectors, guardrail, she knows the secret now—don't cough— and it doesn't matter that the dispatcher from the Greyhound station is telling the beefy sheriff how girls come through that station of his at any old hour of the day or night, fifty or a hundred of them in a month sometimes but yeah, he knows the one. "*Said* she was a waitress," the dispatcher says, and the sheriff's pen flies across the page of his blue notebook. "*Said* that's what she was but she didn't fool me. The very minute she starts asking all them questions I knew she was T-for-trouble. I mean, a little tramp like that—what's she want with somebody like Lou?"

Behind the dispatcher the red-haired black man nods. "Seen through her right away, myself. Just like a picture window."

The fire trail. Unused in years. But she won't get stuck. Like Richard Petty, like A. J. Foyt, she drops the Mustang into low, spins the steering wheel, headlights poking holes between the trees. Chance would be proud of her, but Mrs. Lomax is looking worried. That nice old lady, she twists her hands, just hates to say it, sheriff, "She seemed like a real nice girl but I've always done my duty and Lou said to let you people know. And she came right out and asked about him.

Chance Griffin, she said, bold as brass, as if I didn't have sense enough to make the connection. Like"—not worried now, but getting mad—"like I wasn't real *smart*, you know. Like I was a hick, and after I'd been so nice to her too!" With a sniff of contempt: "You ought to see her hair. Looks like she used Rit instead of Clairol! I hope you catch her soon," she tells the sheriff. "Thinking she's so good. She shouldn't be allowed to get away with it."

"That's how Chance was himself," says Bucky Rowe. "Arrogant, like. No liking or respect for any of us here. Thought he was too good for us; just couldn't wait to get away. And so we all stand square behind Lou for what he did. Wouldn't a one of us done different under the circumstances."

Miss Rita is the only one who doesn't nod agreement. Goofoff not a crook, he didn't deserve to die. But she has her career to think about. "Well," with a worried look at the bar where the talent scout is waiting—fat, flashy, brassy not classy and sugar there's a difference. The Last Chance Saloon for sure. "Well," she tells the sheriff, "you've got till Tuesday to find her. Crazy kid, she's not dressed for the mountain. She'll have to hole up somewhere and wait for him to come down."

Her lungs are on fire but it's not too bad; headlights still probing the dark spaces between trees, the wrong man is dead; the other sniffs his gun and smiles. "Shh," Hosea tells her. He holds her with his eyes. "Shh," but he doesn't need to say it, he knows where she's been and who with and what doing. Acid. Her brain's a sieve, his eyes are fiery pinwheels that singe her with their sparks. "Shh," but he knows she'll keep quiet, that she doesn't care, that she's just catching her breath here before she takes off again. If he wants to pick Jimmy up in the middle of the night and carry him outside that's all right with her.

That night or the next? Time comes apart. Pieces of her go

with it. Only the essentials remain—she needs to pee. Carefully, holding her head, she gets up. Jimmy Lee's bed is empty, his wagon gone from the porch. At four in the morning? "Jimmy?" she calls. No answer. No moon either, the sun not yet up, but the whole scene seems somehow washed with light. The silhouette of the tool shed stands out boldly against the sky. The rank grass beside the drive shifts from black to silver-white before her eyes, and back again. A heavy dew has fallen. Maybe that's it, she thinks. Dew. And soon it will be dawn. The little fenced-in patch by the front door that Mama calls the lawn is empty of any living thing. She can see that clearly. She can see everything clearly, for miles and miles, it seems, all the way back to the salt marsh—the tough tall grass with the channel running through and the shifting patches of mud and sand. And Jimmy. She can't imagine how he got there but she knows that's where he is, out there in his wagon, the rising tide eating its way toward him across the sand.

She shouldn't have left him. She shouldn't ever leave him; he knows when she is gone. "Jimmy!" Her voice silences the frogs. Next time she'll take him with her. They'll take the Getaway Road and go to Disneyland.

"Jimmy!" Bats dart, black and silent in the eerie silver light. He knows. He has gone after her. On his own—Jimmy Lee, who can't find the bathroom without help! He has gone after her. She should never have left! Oh, let him be safe and she'll never leave again!

"Jimmy!" splashing through the shallows, dancing from one firm spot to the next, no need to plan or think. She knows the marsh better than she knows her bedroom. Weeds clutch at her ankles; firm sand then yielding mud then sand again exactly where it should be. But the channel betrays her. "Jimmy!" as the sand gives way suddenly and she plunges forward, slow-moving water closing over her head.

Bones. At the bottom of a deep, deep pool her groping

fingers touch them and she jerks her hand away. She surfaces, gasping and spitting. Strings of weed slide down her cheeks. *"Jimmy!"* He is here. He is here. He has to be. She rolls over and dives, clawing among rotten submerged branches and old tires to find the mossy ribcage, the smooth pelvis, the cow's skull with weed hanging like dark snot from the place where its nostrils had been when she brings it to the surface. She flings it away in disgust, gulps air, goes under again. More ribs, a spine. Weeds like old men's slimy fingers brush her face and the blood roars in her ears. But on her way up again her foot bumps against something that feels like, that has to be, metal. One more deep breath and down again, groping and pawing—a wheel! A front wheel, it has to be! and the wagon's handle and then Jimmy Lee's bare foot. And he's alive! She feels him move, the faintest twitch but it's enough. She grabs his leg, grabs him by the waistband of his shorts, by his hair—*Jimmy!*—and with the last of her strength pushes off from the muddy bottom. Up they float. She sees the moon, a faint yellow blob, its soft rim crumbling and wavering. Jimmy Lee floats gently beside her. Weightless. His pale face soft and formless as the moon. Her brother. She loves him, he is the only thing she loves but he is breaking up, breaking up, the current pulling at him now. It has grown stronger, dragging his mouth open and peeling his lips back from his teeth. Somehow they have gotten into the main channel. It has hold of them, it has hold of Jimmy and threatens to suck him loose from her grasp. And it is taking forever to reach the surface and she knows for certain now that they both will drown.

Kicking feebly, clutching his hair, she wills him: Jimmy, you got to help! And she can feel him trying, waving his arms; his legs flutter in the rushing current like pennants in the wind but it is no good. She kicks again. Again. Her legs are rubber. Again. Her lungs burn; there is a squealing in her ears. Red spots dance between her and the waiting moon. Another kick.

A red spot bursts and runs in a crooked dark red line across the sky. It looks like a highway on a map; it draws her to it, the Getaway Road. Leave Jimmy and just go.

Water sears her lungs. The red moon flares. Then her head is above water and she's coughing, coughing, her mouth gritty with sand. She's alive, she's safe, but her hands are empty and Jimmy Lee is gone.

No use to dive again. The current has taken him.

They pulled him up the next day, a mile or so downstream. Not Jimmy Lee at all, some other guy. A stranger. Mexican. Migrant worker or transient; no ID and no one knew his name. All the same, he drew a good-sized crowd.

Ellen stood looking down at him. His mouth was open. Mud coated his tongue and teeth. "Crabs," somebody said, pointing to the ragged eyelids, the tattered lower lip. "He's been dead awhile, that boy."

Three days at least, the coroner said, and later there was trouble. Ellen had to go into Vista Sol to the sheriff's office. They didn't out-and-out accuse her, but she knew they thought she'd killed the man somehow. What had she been doing out there in the marsh at that hour of the night? How had she known where to dive? "I had a sort of a dream," she said, but she had to admit it didn't make sense. "I dreamed my brother was drowning and I had to save him. I saw where to go in the marsh and I went and there he was. Only," shivering, thinking about the little bag of 'ludes in the springs of her bed, "only it wasn't him, it was that other guy. I can't explain it any better than that."

Finally they let her go. Hosea, of all people, gave her an alibi. "Couldn't of been her," he said. "I been watchin' her real tight, and her and some guys was over to the Gulfside Motel all last week." He glared at her across the bare, harshly lit room. "It ain't that I don't think she'd be capable," he told the sheriff. "But this particular time she was just too busy doing other things."

The fire trail ends on a barren rocky bluff. Ellen rolls down the window. The cold wind clears her head. She shivers, breathing carefully through her teeth. "Chance?"

Wind in the trees, the rasping of her breath and then his voice: "Sugar."

She leans out the window but the wind burns her eyes and the clouds gather and he is gone. "I'm going to do it," she says. "One way or another I'm going to get it done."

Wrapped in a beach towel she found in the trunk, she sits on the Mustang's front bumper, watching as the air turns silver and then clears and brightens, and the creek sparkles far below her and the cabin begins to separate itself out of a stand of pines. Before long she can make out the angle of the roof and the glint of light on a windowpane. It is just as he described it: a weathered little shanty with a kind of tower at one end. All that's missing is a feather of blue smoke from the stone chimney.

It is strange how much better she feels, because nothing is really any better at all. But it's as if the sore throat, the burning lungs, the rag-doll knees belong to someone else, some yellow-haired stranger who's stolen a car and a gun and now is making her tottery way down off the ridge, slipping and sliding in her high-heeled boots. *That* girl has a problem. But she, Ellen—watching with some amusement as the yellow-haired one suddenly sprawls forward, rolling and tumbling helplessly until she fetches up against the roots of a gnarled and rough-barked shrub—*she* feels strong and fit.

The footbridge sways under her weight. Below, the creek has almost overrun its banks. It bolts past, yellow-brown with mud, its surface littered with leaves and twigs and strings of dirty foam. The bridge railings are so weathered that she can barely see the carvings. She peels off her gloves and closes her eyes. An owl, yes, and a fish and some kind of antelope or deer. Her fingers find them easily. But when she reaches for her gloves again they have disappeared.

An iced-over path leads from the bridge across the meadow and into the pines. A skin of new snow lies on it, the color of skim milk in the half light under the trees. Ellen squats on her heels for a moment, studying the ground. Squirrel tracks, the scratchings of birds. It isn't hard to imagine that they're the same tracks and scratchings he used to study all those years ago. The very same.

"Sugar, didn't I tell you?"

His voice comes from within her, as if she were actually two people, Chance and Ellen, squatting there. Three people, really: Chance and Ellen and the brassy blonde, all together in one body. She doesn't question how this can be, it simply is, and they crouch in the wet snow, boots soaked, toes going numb and throat burning with a distant fire as they bend down the whiplike saplings and set the snares. Chance says, "Sugar, we got to find us a better gun."

She has to wait while the blond girl fights off a wave of wracking coughs. "I had a forty-four. It's at the hotel, I couldn't get it. But this will do the job." Then, calmly, dropping Miss Rita's pistol back into her purse and pointing toward the cabin, "Look."

The old woman comes slowly down the path, closely followed by a bony shepherd dog. She too is just as he has described. Her sparse hair is white, pulled back into a knob at the nape of her neck. She wears bib overalls and a calfskin jacket shiny with age. A face like oak; she doesn't smile but clearly they are welcome. Clearly she has been waiting for them. She holds out a hard brown hand. "Come inside."

The cabin walls are blank and cold as the ice on the puddles in the path. The front porch sags. An old red metal lawn chair lies rusting on its side by the steps. Jays squabble in the trees and something little and quick—a mouse?—darts from the corner of the porch and disappears under a pile of rocks. There is no sound except the birds, no movement except the mouse, which pops up out of its hole and sits on its haunches, watching. Chance, the old woman and the dog have vanished. Ellen and the blond girl silently enter the cabin.

The main room is a square, roughly twelve by twelve. A dirty sheet curtains off the doorway to the second room; a frail splintery ladder leads to the crow's nest. The cabin is cold and has a musty sour smell, like wet ashes. A wood-burning stove, its door hanging by one hinge, stands on a sheet of blackened tin in one corner. There is a table, heavy and well made, and a rickety store-bought chair. Unpainted pine cupboards on the wall near the stove. Ellen opens them and finds a few thick china cups and plates, a box of rusty forks and spoons, a wooden-handled kitchen knife with the point broken off. A package of Bisquick lies on its side, one corner chewed away and the flour spread all over the shelf, peppered with mouse droppings. A plastic soap dish with a lid contains wooden matches. She scrapes one against the rough surface of the stove. Flame spits and crackles and then holds steady.

It is difficult, in the dim light, to see the paintings on the walls and rafters. She lights another match: deer, a leaping fish, an eagle with outstretched wings. Black, red and brown, mottled with shadows, just barely visible under the layers of greasy soot and grime.

A jar of instant coffee stands on the table, two-thirds full, and the coffee smells fresh. There is water in the kettle on the stove; the kettle's sides are bright with fine fresh scratches as if it has been recently scoured. Ellen builds a small fire in the stove and continues her search of the cabin while the water heats.

The dirty sheet in the doorway feels greasy and stinks of mildew and old smoke. The second room is tiny. Closet-sized. Dark. She strikes another match: narrow iron bed with no mattress. Chest of drawers. The stub of a dirty white candle on the chest is glued there by a ring of its own wax. She scrapes the foul damp wick with her nails; it takes flame just as the match is about to burn her fingers.

The top drawer is empty except for a gray sweater, one sleeve half eaten by moths. She puts it on. It is a good thick sweater and she is cold. The second drawer is empty, period. In the third, more mouse droppings and a box of shotgun shells.

Cobwebs in one corner of the room sway a little although she can feel no draft. A yellow and green cat's-eye marble on the floor is wedged so firmly between two planks that she is unable to pry it loose. Dust lies thick on everything. Ellen doesn't see the shotgun right away, and when she does notice the long, burlap-wrapped package leaning in the corner, she doesn't immediately recognize it for what it is—an old twelve-gauge over and under like the one Chance used when he went up to Pennsylvania after deer. She carries it out to the main room where the light is better. It doesn't seem to be missing any parts. She cocks it. Pulls the lead trigger. The hammer falls with a solid, satisfying click.

Behind her, the blond girl slumps shivering at the table, struggling to uncap her bottle of cough medicine. Ellen regards her with contempt. She's an intruder. She's weak. She can ruin everything; she'll have to be dealt with. And what a fool to come up here on the mountain in the high-country cold, where people freeze to death even in September, dressed the way she is. Ellen shakes her head. For sure she'll have to be dealt with, but not now.

For now the important thing is the shotgun. Ellen cradles it against her chest. She understands that all along she has known it would be here, that it is part of the plan. The cabin not the ranch, not Tuesday night but now, so that Chance will be with her; so that she can close her eyes and see every bare twig, every blade of frost-scorched grass and patch of snow; see the sun glittering on a vein of fool's gold in the rock they will be hidden behind. She and Chance together, as they should be. She feels the hard cold ground beneath her knees and the rough sun-warmed rock against her cheek and the weight of the shotgun dragging against her arm. They are high on the mountainside, just below the treeline with an open valley spreading out below them. All around them are gray rocks, granite laced with iron pyrite and crusted with lichens. Low bushes grow nearby: juniper and mesquite, and twisted, stunted pines. They can see a long way in both directions up and down the valley and have an excellent view of the rugged slopes beyond. But that is of little importance. They know exactly which way Lou French will come.

They have tracked him only long enough to be sure, waiting in the predawn cold, watching as the men come laughing and joking and cursing from the lodge, God damn! you *know* it's wicked out here! Watching the hired hands bring the saddles from the lean-to and sling them onto the corral fence near where the horses and mules are finishing their hay, tied up in a row like laundry on a line. Then the sun rolls a little higher and the shadows roll back a little more and a kind of gauzy silver light touches the other paddock and silhouettes a Thoroughbred mare, heavy in foal. "Look there," Ellen says. "I knew it all along."

Chance makes no response. Perhaps he has climbed higher

on the hillside for a better view. No matter, he'll be back. She still can feel his presence as she presses close against the trunk of a gnarled old pine, breathing lightly so as not to cough as the ranch hands rig the packs on the mules and saddle the horses for the hunters. Lou French tacks up his own mount, a sturdy roan. She hasn't seen him for a long time now, but she would know him anywhere. Even in the half-dark, moving in and out of the shadows. No mistake. She has him memorized.

You're a dead man, she tells him silently. It won't be long now.

That night she settles behind a patch of brambles that reach out across a stream, leaning the shotgun barrel carefully against a rock and watching the cook prepare the hunters' meal. Big cuts of meat, potatoes in the coals. A few dry withered berries cling to the brambles. She strips them into her mouth, one or two at a time; crunches them, seeds and sweetness, while she watches the men gather around their fire, plates in their laps, knives and forks in their hands, napkins tucked into their shirts or belts, and there is salt and pepper, there is ketchup, there are pickles and sliced onions and a bottle of the good stuff to wash it down. She hears their laughter; it rises like mist out of the canyon as the light fails and the cook throws another log on the fire. The wind snatches the yellow flames and twists the men's long shadows into crooked shapes as they sit down in a circle on the stones and stumps with their plates on their knees. The doctors and congressmen look like good boys on a camp-out in their stiff new jeans and fleece-lined jackets— the way they laugh and joke as the bottle makes the rounds. But looks can deceive; they wield their forks like weapons. In the bouncing firelight their knifeblades flash and the meat they lift to their mouths drips red and stains their lips and teeth.

Lou French has already drawn apart. Already he is preparing himself; he has not drunk any of the whiskey, but merely raised the bottle to his lips and pretended to swallow. He sets his plate aside, his food untouched. She watches as he excuses himself, "got to check the mules," and slips from the circle of light into the shadows. Indistinct, a shadow himself, he makes his way past the corral to the creek. There he kneels, cups his hands and drinks.

The nape of his neck glows pale against the dark of his red-plaid hunter's cap and the dark of his jacket and the dark of the night. The shotgun is within easy reach but Ellen merely makes a gun of her thumb and forefinger, tracking him as he straightens, wipes his mouth on his sleeve, walks some distance from the creek and pees against a slab of rock. His urine smokes in the cold air; the smell stays strong, despite the dirt he scuffs around, the juniper needles he scatters.

He continues on, walking beside the creek. The banks are overgrown with berry canes. Even in the dark she can see the berries clinging, see his hand reach out, his fingers pluck. He has many more berries available to him than she does, but he is preparing himself; he knows, he knows, and takes only a few. He eats them slowly. Ellen takes another handful too; together they dine on berries hard as bullets. She puts her finger into the creek and a moment later he bends down, not cupping his hands this time but placing his lips against the surface of the water like a kiss, and drinks, and she knows then that he is hers. That he is theirs. She can leave now and sleep in comfort in the cabin, she and Chance together, and tomorrow they will find him. No. He will find them. Come to them. They have only to wait.

The water on the stove is boiling. Ellen sets the old gun on the table and makes a cup of coffee. There's even a jar of Cremora. Here, she says, and the blond girl reaches eagerly, needing the warmth. But her hand shakes; the cup clatters to the tabletop, rolls crookedly to the edge and drops. Ellen picks it up: not damaged so she refills it, but the other girl has at last succeeded in removing the cap from the codeine bottle and is drinking that instead. It seems to help. When Ellen mounts the ladder to the crow's nest her yellow-haired shadow is close behind.

Ellen isn't sure what she expected. An easel or table, maybe; a sturdy oak table with a sketchbook open to the half-completed drawing of a mountain lion, and some carvings, his as well as his grandmother's. That's what she would have liked. Fresh wood scraps on the floor as if they've both been working there all day, have just stepped out and will be back at any moment. Instead, Ray and Angie Vincent are complaining that she, no, that the yellow-haired one was ungrateful, that she was hard and unfeeling. After all we did for her, they say, and the blond girl coughs and coughs. Poor thing, thinks Ellen. She knows she should do something, try to help, but later. Now she gazes about the empty room. Sketchbook? Carvings? Even the stub of a pencil would do; something he might have used. No luck. Nothing but dust and, in one corner, some drifted leaves.

She goes to the front window. There is a good view up and down the valley. Clouds are piling up again, pale gray and swollen, so low above the ridge that they obscure the tips of the tallest trees. On the bluff, touched by a stray beam of sun, the pink Mustang shimmers like a neon sign: GLORIOUS BLOOD REVIVAL. And Mama asks what does she mean she was looking for Jimmy when everybody knew Hosea had taken him to the meeting. "It was going to be the night when my miracle would happen!" she hisses through clenched teeth. So mad she's shaking; cheeks red with rage instead of rouge. "It was going to happen at last, you could feel it in the air!" she says. "You could see it in Hosea's eyes! The spirit was in him; it was like Nashville all over again." She folds her arms and turns away. "I could feel the power building and building," she tells Ellen.

"Everybody could, even the ones who doubted him. And then I felt it go. Just go, in an instant. Like air out of a balloon."

Mama turns again, facing Ellen, her eyes as cold as winter stars. "I don't want to know what was going on between you and that *pachuc'*. I don't want to hear what happened. Maybe it was justified, maybe he pulled a knife, a Mexican will do that."

"I didn't do *anything!*" Ellen protests. "I thought it was Jimmy in the marsh! I was trying to save him."

"Only one way you can save that boy," Mama says. "And that's to get out of his life. The Devil's got his eye on you; you better pack your stuff and just go."

So she had left, for good that time; just the one trip back, old T-for-trouble with its tricky currents and its bones. The salt marsh, she thinks now. A good place to dump Lou French, but the mountain will have to do. And tomorrow he will come to her. To them. They have only to wait.

Ellen watches as the blond girl lowers herself onto the bed of leaves. Weak. Unfit to travel. She could ruin everything, she'll have to be dealt with. Ellen thinks of herself at the Vincents' bathroom mirror, making a pistol of her finger. She could have done it then. It shouldn't be hard now. You did what you had to do.

Distant voices rouse her and she climbs painfully to her feet, hooking an elbow over the windowsill to haul herself up. Aside from being stiff and weak she doesn't feel too bad. Her throat doesn't hurt at all, her eyes stay focused on whatever she aims them at, and she can breathe without setting off the colored lights. But she has the unsettled feeling of having been away somewhere, not just asleep, for a lengthy but indefinite period of time. It seems to be a clear, fine evening: Saturday? Tuesday? She has no idea, but takes comfort in the fact that the Mustang is still there on the bluff. Surely, if *too* many days had passed someone would have found it. Wouldn't they? And her as well?

Ellen looks at the car. It stands in shadow, an almost-neutral rosy tan. Only the curve of the roof still catches the sun and blazes away, a ruddy pink like the top of a bald man's sunburned head. Voices again. Men—a good-sized group from the sound of things, and the mournful braying of a mule. She leans out the window as far as she dares, but can see nothing. The other three windows are shuttered. Two of them have been nailed, but the third gives under her hand when she undoes the latch. The hinges squeal; the sound startles her and she stands very still for several minutes, listening. The mule brays again, closer but not much.

The shutter won't open all the way, but she shoves it far enough that she can see the lower end of the canyon and Copper Creek sliding among granite boulders in a series of deep bends. She can see the riders coming, a little band of five or six, and pack mules loaded with bulky gear, winding their way single file through the trees, down a rocky trail from the ridge to the canyon floor. At the foot of the ridge they disappear into a dense grove of pines, emerging a few minutes later one by one out of the blue shadows into the fading light.

One man, two, three; the fourth rider leads a reluctant mule. Another two riders, more mules, gutted deer strapped to their pack frames. Lou French himself brings up the rear.

Tired, relaxed, successful, their guard down—maybe a little drunk?—they jog steadily up the canyon, glancing neither right nor left as they pass the cabin, the bridge and the one-way trail of her footprints in the mud and melting snow, while high on the bluff above them the pink Mustang sinks deeper into shadow, a colorless shape like a big square-cornered rock except for the last few brilliant inches—no more than a hand span, surely—of the roof.

Lou French drops back a little from the group, sweeping

the canyon with his green-eyed gaze. She sees him stiffen, his face turned toward the bluff. The Mustang is completely shadowed; no longer pink at all, but definitely a car. "Hey!" His voice carries faintly over the sound of hooves on stones and the rushing of the creek. The other riders halt, rein their horses around to look where he is pointing. They stand in their stirrups, steadying themselves on the horns of their saddles as Lou French points to the car again, and to the line of footprints and finally to the cabin.

And then they ride on. All but Lou French, who urges his horse up the path toward the cabin.

Her prey. Coming to her, coming within range of even Miss Rita's little gun, which she takes from her purse and holds lightly in her hand. Surprise on her side, she can have him now, or she can call to him, please help me, her only chance (a part of her clearly understands) to get down out of here alive. Make up your mind, she tells herself, and she sees the Eustice brothers, poor drunk country boys with nothing better to do on a Saturday night than roll dice to find out who to kill.

Lou French rides toward the cabin. Not his jet, they burned him good, just took him to the cleaners. That was it. She believes that was it; that was what happened when you did business with A-rabs; there's no doubt in her mind. And it's okay. That's life, a crazy crapshoot after all. She spins the pistol once on her finger, takes aim at the trapdoor where his head will appear. Then she breaks the gun open, shakes the bullets out and wedges them carefully, all but one, into a crack between two boards in the wall beside the window. She replaces the remaining bullet in the chamber, she isn't sure why, and gives the cylinder a Hollywood cowboy spin. We're all of us killers, maybe, one time in six. "Mr. French!" she calls. A moment later she hears him on the porch. The door creaks. Silence, but she knows he is inside now, listening, searching the room, reading all the signs. Ransacked drawers, used cup and pan. Shotgun and shells on the table where she left them.

And then he is moving again, very cautiously it seems, but a board squeaks and she hears him breathing or thinks she can, and the soft shuffle of his feet on the dirty floor as he approaches the stove, moves to the threshold of the second room and then to the foot of the ladder.

"Hello?" he says quietly. It isn't really a question; he knows she is there. "Are you okay? Do you need any help?" Climbing now, the flimsy ladder trembling under his weight. His head appears in the trapdoor, gray hair almost white in the dimness of the room, and then his shoulders; one hand and then another. She holds him in her sights for a moment, then puts the gun in her pocket.

"Over here."

He doesn't jump or flinch but merely turns his head, squinting at her as she stands at the front window with the sunset at her back. "My God," after the briefest hesitation. "It's . . . Ellen, right? Chance's friend. What on earth are you doing here?"

Her hand in her pocket closes around the barrel of the gun. "I'm on my way to California and I wanted to see the cabin and all." Indicating the bluff through the window. "I met Rita. She lent me her car."

He stands on the ladder, leaning through the trapdoor with his weight on his elbows, looking at her in a speculative way. She realizes that she still clutches the pistol, her whole arm unnaturally rigid with tension, and she makes herself let go. Both hands in the open, just as his own are. He asks again, "Are you okay? You don't look exactly the way I remembered you."

"Dyed my hair," she says, "that's all," and it is all. Whatever was wrong with her—bad cold, pneumonia, flu—has cured itself, she'll get down off the mountain just fine without his help. Still, she isn't sorry she called to him. A nice man. Decent. Everybody says so; she thinks so herself. It's hard to believe anyone could take him to the cleaners, but they did. She believes that with all her heart. She says, "How do you like me as a blonde?"

His teeth flash in a smile. "If you were my daughter I'd wring your neck." Then he asks how she is getting along, seems genuinely interested in her job in California, just a real nice guy who'd tried to help a friend.

"I know you weren't selling ringers," she tells him. "And I know you didn't have Chance killed."

He smiles, a little sadly. "And I know you didn't really mean that dream you had about me."

"That's right," she says, as a back corner of her mind wonders dimly how he knew about that when she'd never told a soul. "Chance was my one and only," she says, and she knows it's true. She hadn't really wanted that dream, that life. It was just silliness; she'd been flattered by his attention; it was just a little crush, that's all.

Lou French raises his left wrist close to his face to read his watch. Below them his horse paws impatiently, its hooves scraping the stony ground. "I'd better head on; I'm going to lose my light. You sure you don't need any help?"

"I'm fine," she tells him. "Perfect. No problem. And I better go too, or Rita'll have the sheriff out looking for me." She puts out her hand. "Thanks for stopping. I'm really glad I saw you again."

His hand is warm, firm and dry, callused, as Chance's had been. "Write me a note," he says. "Let me know how you like California."

"Will do," although she knows she won't. She watches him ride off up the canyon, a tough spare man, not too tall, on a roan horse, growing smaller and smaller in the twilight until he disappears. And she thinks of Gene Rumstead, of his acne-scarred cheeks and nice smile. He never called the sheriff on her; nobody called the sheriff on her. The sheriff was in the Aberdeen on business of his own.

Don't go. Gene doesn't say it, not out loud, but she knows somehow it's on his mind. Don't go, but she has to go. Job waiting in Turlock, but maybe she'll come back one day. Vacation in Reno. He'll drive up to meet her, he says. And she believes that he will.

The blond girl's teeth chatter against the mouth of the codeine bottle. Ellen knows she should help her, and she will. Soon. Any minute now. But she looks out the window at Copper Creek, mud-brown and gleaming, and she sees the other creek too, where Chance will be waiting, and the broad grassy valley that is the place where it will end. First things first. That girl isn't going anywhere.

The valley is exactly as she knew it would be. Still, she checks it thoroughly, moving quickly from tree to boulder to clump of brush, scuttling like a lizard where the cover is thin. She stays among the rocks and brush; she leaves no trail, but there are deer tracks in the patches of wet bare earth that she avoids, and deer droppings and the droppings of bear. Within an hour she is satisfied that she knows the valley as well as she needs to know it. She finds more berry bushes and fills her pockets. Chance is nowhere around. She crouches behind a rock to wait for him. For both of them.

The sun climbs and begins to drop again. Her legs grow numb with cold and cramped from waiting, from not moving. Her fingers are stiff; she has no gloves. From time to time she touches the shotgun's worn stock for reassurance.

And he is there. Not Chance—Lou French, too soon! She can't see him; he hasn't left the trees, but she feels his presence, a disturbance in the air, some subtle change. And then she hears the soft thud of his horse's hooves on the pine needles, the snap of a dead branch, the creak of his saddle as he reins to a halt and stands in his stirrups, peering out of the shadows into the icy glare of the late-afternoon sun. She smells his sweat; he knows, he knows. He would like to turn away. Instead, he settles back into his saddle, loosens his rifle in its sling and rides on.

He enters the valley perhaps a quarter mile downwind of where she waits. Ellen notes how his nostrils flare and his cool eyes search the meadow ahead of him and travel slowly up the valley wall.

Her hands are warm now, even a little sweaty, no longer stiff. The heavy gun seems weightless. Lou French legs his horse northward, riding slowly closer, scanning the meadow and the valley wall. She eases the safety off and thumbs the hammers. There is no scope on the old gun, but even without, his face looms huge in the V notch of the sights. Like a landscape: each eye a cool green lake, his nose a rocky crag above twin caves. Forehead and cheeks broad as rolling rangeland, his mouth the parched banks of a dry stream, teeth like boulders. Quartz. They glitter as he smiles.

His eyes rake the valley left and right. He has begun to whistle. She lowers the gun, she can't say why, then jerks it to her shoulder again. But still she doesn't fire. Where is Chance? He should be with her; this means nothing without him. Lou French rides on. He whistles softly. And then, still whistling, he lifts the thirty-thirty from its leather sling in front of his right thigh and looks up, probing the mountainside— boulders, loose stones, patches of scrub. Ellen sights down the long nose of the shotgun, locked into the tunnel of his right ear, willing him to turn, to raise his eyes, to look at her as she rises to her feet behind the wall of rock and juniper. She wants him to see her. She wants to see him when he sees.

And she wants Chance there. More than she has ever wanted anything, it seems, she wants Chance with her and she wants that last half-second for the three of them.

Too late. Chance doesn't come; Lou French doesn't turn, he rides on by, easy in the saddle now, his roan horse loping, hooves clattering on the stones. Going away from her—he knows, he knows!—and he offers his back, broad as a continent. She can't miss. No one could miss. But the gun barrel shakes; it has a life and fights her, drawing circles and figure eights and lopsided eggs on the clear bright air. Her hands sweat again and her arms throb with exhaustion; she lacks sufficient strength to squeeze the trigger. When she finally does fire the gun it is with her eyes tight shut, the barrel aimed at the sky.

No.

Too late. He doesn't turn, he rides on by, his roan horse loping. Going away; he knows, he knows, and offers his back broad as a continent. She can't, no one could, the gun barrel holds steady; it has a life and quiets her, absorbs her shaking, holds like a magnet to a spot between his shoulder blades. She squeezes the trigger. Click.

Again.

He lopes on by, going away, he knows, he offers his back. Broad as a continent, a map of North America: Cresta, Nevada; Florida; Virginia and Scott's Run. Galveston, T-for-trouble, the salt marsh, all of the roads between them drawn down into a tiny spot between his shoulder blades. Bullfrog and fly: *snap*. Ellen squeezes the trigger. The old gun's roar fills the valley as his jacket explodes.

Blue nylon, white goose down, red goose down in wet clumps; he flings up his arms, his head snaps back. Then, somehow he clutches the saddle horn, claps spurs to his horse's sides and races towards the trees.

Pure reflex. She knows that. There is no urgency, no need to hurry. Lou French is a dead man. He won't go far.

But he is tough and travels farther than she would have believed possible—more than a mile on a galloping horse with his back half blown away. In a way she is pleased; she is almost proud, as if somehow she too has performed this feat of endurance, undergone this ordeal with such courage and determination.

He is still breathing when she reaches him. Not conscious, but breathing. He lies on his back in a sandy gully at the foot of a steep stretch of boulders, loose stones and bleached broken branches. One leg twisted beneath him and his arms flung wide. A trail of crimson smears shows where he fell and slid and rolled. His face is scratched. He wears a three-day stubble which for some reason sends a pang through her; she remembers his silk handkerchief, his soft tweed coat. Like something in a magazine. His hands are scraped. Blood wells from his nose and his right ear. His roan horse stands, reins trailing, on the rocky path above them.

Ellen approaches him cautiously. She half expects that at any moment he may jump up and run away, jump up and attack her; that he may vanish into thin air or sink out of sight, swallowed up by the sand that shifts and whispers beneath her boots as she walks toward him. But he stays put. She kneels and leans down with her face next to his. He breathes rapidly, through his mouth. She stares at his lips, cracked and chapped as her own are from the cold. His warm breath fans her cheek. Once. Twice.

"Mr. French!" she says. She wants him to know. "We're here," she tells him, although she is alone. "You had it coming, and we came."

A tremor shakes him, a hard, shuddering spasm, and he goes rigid and arches his back and snores once deep in his throat. His right hand lifts, one finger extended; he looks at her. Through her and then at her, his cracked lips draw back into something like a smile. Then his hand drops. He scrabbles for a moment, then lies still among the loose stones and the weathered broken branches that Ellen sees now are not branches at all but bones. A horse's skeleton, not complete—parts have been dragged away by coyotes, perhaps, or bear. But she can see the spine, the curving pelvis, teeth scattered like pebbles, and there among the teeth something that looks at first a little like a tooth but is not.

Carefully she reaches out with a hand now clumsy and thick-fingered with cold, and plucks it from among the pebbles: a tiny delicate foal's hoof like a shell, like something Chance might have carved. She puts it in her pocket and she closes Lou French's eyes and wipes the blood from his face as best she can with the sleeve of the gray sweater. And then she climbs the hill and catches the roan.

It takes a long time to hoist the dead man onto the horse's back, but she manages, tying him in place with the sweater, knotting one sleeve around one of his wrists, passing the body of the sweater under the girth and knotting the other sleeve to his belt, which she has looped around his feet. And then, because her clothes are soaked and she is cold, she shoves her hands into the dry gloves she finds in his pocket. She places his red-plaid hunter's cap on her head and takes the woolen scarf, still warm, from his neck. And then she starts off, leading the roan horse slowly down the mountain over the broken rocky ground.

11

THE OLD WOMAN sits cross-legged in the semidarkness outside
the circle of light cast by the kerosene lamp. She doesn't speak
when they come in, stamping snow and chunks of frozen mud
from their boots, but nods toward the stove where a fire is
dying to embers under a black kettle and the coffeepot. A
single place—thick, chipped white china plate, red plastic mug,
bent-handled spoon—has been laid at the table. Chance peels
off his red jacket, tosses his old gray Stetson onto the back of
a chair, sits down at the table without a word and eats hungrily
when Ellen fills his plate. Pink beans, chilis and onions, and
thick slices of fat bacon; he wipes up the juice with a heel of
coarse dry bread while she watches him fondly. He is there
with her. Not just a voice or a presence, a piece, a sketch, but
the man himself come home at last. His cheek when she touches
it is warm, solid, rough with stubble. She puts her fingers on
his throat to feel him swallow. He stops chewing, looks at her
quizzically with his clear blue eyes while she studies him:
angle of cheek and chin, pink soft complicated curve of ear,
like a miracle, she thinks, the lobe covered with blond fuzz.
His hair lies flat against his head. His hat has left a faint red
crease across his forehead.

"You're not eating, sugar." It isn't a question; he adds with a smile, "Bet you'll have a drink with me, though."

"What?" She looks up from stirring the kettle where his second helping of beans is keeping warm, and it seems to her that the old woman chuckles again from the shadows where she sits, wiping the shotgun with an oily rag, the skinny dog beside her.

He grins, showing his strong white teeth. "You better stay away from Rita, sugar. Gal like that can mess you up for sure!" He's joking; he knows full well she never believed a word that Rita or any of the others said.

She laughs and fills his plate again, and when he has eaten she builds up the fire and heats water in the kettle to do the dishes, which she washes with a curled leathery scrap of amber-colored soap. He lights a cigar and smokes it leaning back with his feet in holey blue wool socks parked on the table with the ketchup and bread crumbs and the bottle of Ten High. The smell of tobacco mingles with the smell of wood smoke and gun oil and dog and hot leather as their boots bake beside the stove, and of coffee and fried bacon and the gray-green herbs tied to dry in dusty bunches beneath the rafters. A puff of cold air blows out the candle on the table and flattens the flames in the stove, and when she looks, the shotgun leans in the corner where his grandmother was sitting and Ellen and Chance are alone.

"Come here," he says and holds out his arms. "Sugar, it's been so long." She sits on his thighs, facing him, her knees beside his hips and he is there, bone and ropy muscle, blue veins in his forearms when she pushes up his sleeves, map of blond hair on his chest darkening as it disappears beneath his belt. It feels odd at first to kiss him; she can't get used to all those teeth.

But the rest. The bed made up with thin cotton blankets

instead of sheets because of the chill; lantern on a nail high on the rough-sawn wall, everything so homey and familiar. It is as if they have been away a long time, she and Chance, but this is where they belong. "Just a minute, sugar." No shirt but he zips on the red jacket, takes the lantern and struggles sockless into hot boots to step outside. She waits—what else can she do?—hardly daring to breathe. She knows it will be all right. But she has—they have—come just this far so many times.

Voices in the distance. The blond girl climbs slowly to her knees, crawls to the window and hangs on with both hands as the world shades to black and starts a long slow roll. Voices. Men, she can see them glowing, white figures on dark ground. A good-sized group, they make their way down through the trees to the valley floor. Seven riders, three mules; Lou French himself brings up the rear. Help! the girl cries weakly, help! but they can't hear her above the squeaking of their saddles and the clatter of shod hooves on stone. *Help!* taking off the gray sweater, feebly waving it like a flag.

His shadow in the doorway. His silhouette behind the bed-sheet curtains as he sets the lantern on the table in the other room. And she is suddenly afraid. It will end here, she thinks. So many times it has ended here, with the toilet flushing and the light fanning across the Airstream's ceiling, his silhouette, then nothing. But he is beside her now in the chill smoke-smelling darkness, humming under his breath as he unbuckles his belt, unzips his jeans . . .

> *How many times have you heard someone say*
> *If I had his money I could do things my way*

. . . breaking off for a moment, hopping on one foot—"damn!"—and a boot thunks on the dusty plank floor . . .

CHANCE

But little they know that it's so hard to find
One rich man in a hundred with a satisfied mind

Another pause as the second boot hits the floor, and then the whisper of rough cloth against his hairy thighs. The bedsprings scrinch as he sits down beside her. And he sings—hums, really—

Once I was wading in fortune and fame
Everything I could dream of to get a start in life's game
But suddenly it happened, I lost every dime
But I'm richer by far with a satisfied mind

Smiling, his face just inches from hers . . .

Money can't buy back your youth when you're old
Or a friend when you're lonely or a love that's grown cold

. . . just inches apart; they breathe each other's breath . . .

But one thing for certain, when it comes my time
I'll leave this old world with a satisfied mind

. . . and she puts her finger to his lips. No. No rich men no poor men, nothing before him, nothing beyond, just one sweaty shoulder and the tip of one ear glowing above her in the lantern light and his butt smooth and tense in her hands before she flings . . .

He sees! Lou French sees her and he sees her tracks shimmering white in the inky snow. Veering off from the group, he rides alone up the path toward the cabin, and she knows that the blond girl, the intruder, is safe. But where *she* is there is neither safety nor danger; there is nothing before and nothing beyond. Just Chance, just a shoulder, a tip of an ear glowing above her and his butt in her hands. Not rich men not poor men, Lou French is a dead man, sugar you and me as she flings her legs around him. And she would hold him that way forever if she could; hold the both of them that way, unchanging and forever, if she could.

A Note About the Author

Sara McAulay was born in Washington, D.C.,
and grew up in Northern Virginia. She is the
author of a previous novel, *Catch Rides*, and a
book for young people, *In Search of the Petroglyph*.
Ms. McAulay lived for many years in the San
Francisco Bay area but now lives in New Jersey.

A NOTE ON THE TYPE

This book was set via computer-driven cathode-ray tube in Janson, a redrawing of type cast from matrices long thought to have been made by the Dutchman Anton Janson, who was a practicing type founder in Leipzig during the years 1668–87. However, it has been conclusively demonstrated that these types are actually the work of Nicholas Kis (1650–1702), a Hungarian, who most probably learned his trade from the master Dutch type founder Dirk Voskens. The type is an excellent example of the influential and sturdy Dutch types that prevailed in England up to the time William Caslon developed his own incomparable designs from them.

Composed by
Crane Typesetting Service, Inc.
Barnstable, Massachusetts

Printed and bound by
Haddon Craftsmen, Inc.
Scranton, Pennsylvania

Book design by Judith Henry